Finding The Field of Favor

Dr. Jerry A. Grillo, Jr.

FINDING THE FIELD OF FAVOR

All scriptures, unless indicated, are taken from the King James Version.

Scripture quotations marked NKJV are taken from the New King James Version.

Scripture quotations marked NIV are taken from New International Version.

ISBN: 978-0-9977689-7-8

Print Date: August 4, 2022

TABLE OF CONTENTS

WORD FROM DR. G

Through the Holy Spirit, people have experienced many encounters with the King of Glory. The faith movement, as well as the salvation movement, came by the Spirit of God. And, throughout the Church's history, there have been many outpourings of distinct touches of His Glory. All these encounters and touches have been working for the building-up of His end-time church.

In the last of the last days, I believe we are going to have one last surge of kingdom glory which will bring about the Father's endorsement of the bride of Christ. He is about to, physically, send His son, Jesus, in order to reconnect Him to His bride, the church. However, there are several things that must happen before this encounter can take place.

1. A falling away, or apostasy, of the religious.
2. A surge of hungry people coming into the church. Those who are hungry for Kingdom answers void of religion.
3. God's incredible endorsement. God's gifts and callings are not revocable. Therefore, whatever God endorsees cannot be unendorsed; and
4. A melting away of carnality that reveals the true "sons of God."

Favor Is:
- God's endorsement
- The mercy of God anthropomorphized, or humanized
- The umbilical cord to God's supply
- Enables people to fulfill their destiny
- A privilege
- Everyone is eligible for *Favor*, but many do not qualify
- A seed before it can be a harvest

5

- Can grant access, or connection, to the unqualified; to those not trained
- Will have you driving a new car while someone else makes the payments
- Cannot be bought; however, it can be sought
- Will increase one's money stream. "Money can't buy you *favor*… but *favor* can get you money"
- Can change a medical report
- Can postpone a scheduled storm
- Can protect against an enemy plotting a person's demise

When it comes to seeking the Lord, it is a good practice to seek His hand of holiness in order to qualify for His hand of favor. Also, when seeking Him, be sure what is being sought is spiritual and not material. Solely seeking His hand can be dangerous, however, seeking revelation into the mysteries of God can unlock the King's favor. It is more important to seek the Kingdom's purposes than to seek the King's gifts.

"Now therefore, I pray, if I have found grace (favor) in Your sight, show me now Your way, that I may know You and that I may find grace (favor) in Your sight. And consider that this nation is Your people." (Exodus 33:13 NKJV)

In order to walk in more of the God's favor, it is important to know more of His purpose. In the book of Matthew, He tells us, *"Seek first His Kingdom and His righteousness and all these things will be added unto you."* What things was He talking about? It was food, clothing, shelter, and increase; everything the gentile nations were seeking. Because provision is available in His Kingdom, it is vital to pursue the King in order to obtain what is in His economy. And, by walking according to the precepts and statutes written within the Word of God, favor is a guarantee. So, for the next season, it is important to be in position to receive His endorsement of favor.

Every generation speculates about the authenticity surrounding the God stories written in the Bible. Due to technology, social media, live streaming, and Instagram, the world is changing rapidly. As a result, there is little, if any, interest in Godly principles, precepts, or laws. From the nursery to the pulpit, the Church, as we know it, is going through dramatic, and uncomfortable, changes. Music, along with the entire church service, has changed; the attitudes and interests of the people have also changed. Thankfully, because changes should be made, not all change is bad. Therefore, I am not against change.

If change encompasses the presence, and power, of Holy Spirit, and it does not overshadow the truth, I am for it. When making any change, it is important that revelation be the focus rather than relevance, otherwise, revelation will be lost. The Kingdom of God will never change; therefore, relevance to worldly mindsets and viewpoints will never fit within the Church.

A Generation Crying Out

According to the News, the world is falling apart. There are injustices, divisions, contentions, and rebelliousness bringing unrest to all people. And, unfortunately, the answer to these problems is not found in politics. It is an unequivocal fact that man-made government is ill equipped to solve these issues. However, there is good news, the Kingdom of God is more than capable of resolving every crisis known to man.

Great meetings are also not the answer; however, a great move of Holy Spirit is necessary. I believe there is a generation, a young generation, looking for the Spirit of the Lord. They want more than an individual who can stand, in the pulpit, and teach about what God did in the days of Moses and Elijah. This new generation is asking the question… **"If there is a living God, where is He?"** As a result, when people start searching for God, it begins to ignite a passion and desire to pursue an answer to this question. Due to their willingness to seek Him out, God says, *"if you seek me, you will find me."*

When people begin to hunger for Holy Spirit, it motivates them to look for, ask about, and seek out ways that will cause Him to respond. In the past, with every move of God, people became more and more curious about the Spirit of the Lord. And, because they had grown tired of religion, they began searching for the God of heaven and earth.

The word of God tells us, *"If we seek Him, we Will find Him."* And, when we find Him, we find His favor. This includes:

- His Goodness
- His Mercy
- His Presence
- His Power
- And His Love

God is not hiding from us…

God is not avoiding humanity; on the contrary, He wants everyone to know Him. He wants people to know the power of His resurrection along with the fellowship of His sufferings. He also wants each person to yield to His death. This is hard due to the fact most people only want His blessing, however, *not all are willing to do what it takes to receive the blessing!* Nothing is free. Everything, good or bad, comes with a price. Salvation was not free; it cost God the death of His only Son.

This book, **"Finding the Field of Favor,"** is written to explain how the Body of Christ can grow in its passion for Holy Spirit. This will enable them to mature, and live, in the **FAVOR OF GOD; BECAUSE, WHEN FAVOR COMES, IT WILL MAKE NO SENSE.**

Because believers are God's children, who have inherited certain rights by adoption, He wants to expose them to the fulness of His power. However, He is not going to release all His fulness until they can handle it correctly. This will require understanding the fundamentals of walking with God and moving into the depths of who He is.

It is Your Time

Growth is the ability to adjust; it is the ability to look at situations through different eyes. While children view circumstances through their immediate problems, or desires, mature adults can discern *the bigger picture.*

I have children and now, I have grandchildren. Children and grandchildren both act the same when faced with an unmet desire – screaming, crying, and temper. No matter the environment, they act as though their world is coming to an end. To put it mildly, these are actions prompted by immature thinking. However, adults should understand, delayed gratification is not denial but an expectation for another time. Maturity enables the adult to rationalize and then, come to a different conclusion. This causes the derailment of disappointment. And, instead of screaming, crying, and temper, there is peace through a different perspective.

When I was a child, I talked like a child, I thought like a child, I reasoned like a child. When I became a man, I put childish ways behind me. (1 Cor 13:11-12 NIV)

It is my desire, for the individual reading this book, that you gain a new perspective on life. It is my prayer that you would understand how God has actively worked in your past and that your history does not decide your destiny. But your destiny is decided by the actions taken in your "today." I say, *"I decide the contract."* Every person decides their life; it is not decided by the past, by one's parents, not even friends. Every single, human being is in the driver's seat of their own life. So, it is time to take responsibility, buckle up, and create a new destiny.

Chapter 1

Process Brings Change

Life is Process

Process is defined as a series of actions, or steps, taken to achieve a particular result; it is living out various stages. It is the daily practice, of a routine, until progress is achieved. Without process:

- There is no life
- There is no success
- There is no victory

Life is process! *Nothing more and nothing less.*

"Success is not a destination... success is a journey"
(John Maxwell).

Life is described in this same way, *"Life is not a destination; it is a journey."* Life is made up of good days and bad days. It is made up of seconds, minutes, hours, days, months, and years; it is full of millions of moments. People do not live from day to day but from moment to moment. Life has its ups and downs as well as its ins and outs. In life, there are good moments and there are bad moments. And, with maturity, the bad moments are prevented from ruining all other moments. Life happens! Life is always happening, even in bad times. So, in the not so good times, remember to avoid placing too much emphasis on Satan. Removing this unnecessary focus will free people from all kinds of stress and its related illnesses. Life is good! And true freedom happens when people decide to glorify God during the process of fulfilling of their God-given assignments.

Life is living, and fulfilling, the daily process leading into one's destiny.

Process is key!
Joy is living life and accepting the changes that occur because of struggles and victories. If people mess up today, there are steps that will help them get up tomorrow. It is the process that separates people from the animal kingdom. People could make changes without anyone telling them. As a result, they are always in the process of attaining the next level of promotion. And, through implementation, progress is unlocked. What is process? *Process* is a series of actions or steps taken to achieve a particular end. Words that describe "process" include procedure, operation, action, activity, exercise, affair, business, job, task, and understanding. Process means system, and when the right systems are discovered, people can walk in success while unlocking divine favor. Every endeavor on earth has a system built into it.

System is, "a set of things working together as parts of a mechanism or an interconnecting network." Order, arrangement, network, and administration are words that help describe a system. So, process is the <u>system</u> for progress."

Favor is not a random event or a moment of luck. It is a divine system, of process, set up by God, for man.

Favor is Process

God Created the World Through Process

God works through a progression of events to establish His finished work. In Genesis, chapter one, God established process when He created the world in seven days rather than in moments. He could have spoken everything into existence with one powerful word, however, the process enabled Him to enjoy the work of creation until its completion. It is not bad having incomplete tasks, journeys, dreams, or accomplishments. And, people can still find satisfaction, and joy, even though the day ended without accomplishing what was intended. The point is, everything cannot be completed in a day; and, that is okay. There is still meaning, in the day, though the project was not completed as expected. Even God, at the end of every day, declared, *"it was good."* Though creation was not finished, He rested in the fact, what He had done was good. And, He knew that the process would bring Him to His desired end; one day at a time. So, enjoy the journey. Enjoy each day as completion of that project looms on the horizon. Take pride in the accomplishments of each day and do not allow failed expectations to negatively alter the value and purpose of the day. Evaluate every decision through the eyes of process, understanding that tomorrow is another day to move closer to the finish line. Find joy, in the journey, knowing that God is patient with our incompletions.

"... being confident of this, that he who began a good work in you will carry it on to completion until the day of Christ Jesus." (Phil 1:5-6 NIV)

Purpose creates value. One of the biggest mistakes in defining purpose is that performance is attached to it. When people allow purpose to be defined by performance, they measure it by the level of performance and not by value. When this happens, people tend to compare what they do with another person's performance. As a result, there is a misinterpretation of purpose based on another's accomplishments; this can cause feelings void of purpose. When people walk this path, it leads into the trap of comparing and competing, with others, for better performance. Purpose is not performance. Purpose is value. More importantly, people have value. When people understand their purpose, their value will begin to create volume. And, it is important to avoid living for volume and live for value instead. It is also essential to celebrate those who are succeeding; admire them because no individual person is less valuable than another. Eventually, people will attract what they admire which brings reward. Therefore, anything that goes uncelebrated, goes unrewarded and will, eventually, exit a person's life.

The power of purpose is understanding that value is not attached to performance. However, success is decided on performance and does not change the person's value. God places value on life and He places favor on the willingness to obey His divine instructions.

Conformity Stops Process

There are many things that keep people from walking in divine favor including: fear, worry, anger, unbelief, doubt, addictions, sexual immorality, along with many other works of the flesh. For believers to gain a level of freedom from these things, they must stop conforming to the patterns dictated by a worldly system. They must be transformed by the renewing of their minds.

Do not conform any longer to the pattern of this world but be transformed by the renewing of your mind. Then you will be able to test and approve what God's will is-his good, pleasing and perfect will. (Rom 12:2. NIV)

Conformity means to behave according to socially acceptable conventions or standards. It means to be similar in form or type; or, to agree. Paul is telling us to stop behaving according to the socially acceptable standards of the culture; instead, be Kingdom minded. All worldly mindsets must be replaced with His Kingdom mentality. At **ChurchOne80**, our motto is, **"Kingdom above everything."** Sticking to this mindset will cause the body of Christ to stand out rather than appearing as though walking in the same darkness as the world. *Romans 12:2 says, "Do not conform to the pattern of this world."* Therefore, living a compromised lifestyle must stop. Believers are people of the light and must live as such. Because the Kingdom of God is a kingdom of light, the Church is no longer to conform to the prevailing standards, attitudes, or practices of a fallen system. If the Church is compromised, how can it be the light the world needs? The Church is here to show a different way, a way of love and obedience to a good God. It has been commissioned to be different to lead others out of a broken system. However, if its understanding has been darkened by deception, it is not able to do that. I command Light to shine upon the Church; His divine light which enables all believers to walk uncompromised, by darkness, as well as to live the life of uncommon favor.

Transformed

Paul not only tells us not to conform but he also tells us to be transformed by the renewing of our minds. *Transformed* means to make a thorough, or dramatic, change in the form, appearance, or character of a thing. Basically, this means a metamorphosis from one thing to another. In people, this is done through the power of thought, or the renewing of the mind. In other words, take that stinking thinking and replace it with God's Word. This will enable the believer to understand God's good, pleasing, and perfect will. However, transformation will not take place if the focus lands on lifestyle rather than on how one thinks. By adapting our minds to new, life-giving thoughts, our lifestyle will change as well. 2 Corinthians 5:17 states, *"Therefore, if anyone is in Christ, the <u>new creation</u> has come: <u>The old has gone</u>, the new is here!"*

Transformation starts with a change of mind before anything can occur in life-experiences. In other words, before people can see a change on the outside, there needs to be a change on the inside first. This is done by taking the Word of God and applying it to the mind, will, and emotions until it becomes stronger than the old carnal thoughts. Paul tells us to renew our minds or make them new again. That does not mean to get a new mind, but a new way of thinking. Paul is telling people to wake up the mind given to them before being formed in their mother's womb.

"Before I formed you in the womb, I knew you, before you were born, I set you apart; I appointed you as a prophet to the nations." (Jeremiah 1:5 NIV)

Unfortunately, from an early age, people are programed to believe their experiences limit them. And the negative words spoken over them have had a detrimental effect on how they view themselves. In other words, the life most people live is based on the realities of their past experiences rather than on the truth of what God says they can be or have. Though all these experiences are real and have shaped the concepts of who people are, His spiritual reality is more real and able to reshape humans into who He sees them to be. However, in general, they have been conditioned to see the natural world which, then, blinds them to the realities of the Spirit realm. Regrettably, the Church seems to focus more on external numbers than on internal awakening. This outward drive for large church gatherings has hindered many from understanding who they are in Christ. There must be an atmosphere shift; one that enables the people to reconcile their past from their present. It would be good to move away from entertaining people and, instead, teaching scriptural principles that help in the renewing of the mind. Some of those principles include:

1. *Conviction:* This happens when the Holy Spirit begins to challenge wrong thinking and wrong actions. He does this through Biblical scriptures which teach, correct, rebuke, and reprove. Once a person understands how they have missed the mark, then their mind can be changed.

2. *Repentance:* This is the next step after conviction. It is a sincere turning away in both the mind and the heart, or from self to God. It involves a change of mind that leads to action – the radical turning away from a sinful course to God.

3. *Confession:* This comes after Holy Spirit conviction and repentance. It is an acknowledging of, or taking responsibility for, one's sins against God. It is a reconciling, to God, through Jesus Christ our Lord. *"...that if you confess with your mouth the Lord Jesus and believe in your heart that God has raised Him from the dead, you will be saved." For with the heart one believes unto righteousness, and with the mouth confession is made unto salvation." (Romans 10:9,10 NKJV)*

4. *Conceiving*: This step involves receiving Holy Spirit. It enables a believer to grow in the grace and

knowledge of the Lord Jesus Christ which brings maturity to the Body of Christ. In addition, the Holy Spirit leads us into all truth, He teaches us all things and is always revealing Jesus. Through Him, we receive power, purpose, as well as the strategies of the King. And it is important to remember, even as Mary conceived Jesus through the supernatural power of Holy Spirit, she also had to carry that pregnancy to term and, then, deliver him. As the Body of Christ, we carry the seed of life within us as well. By Holy Spirit, we must also carry His seed to term, then, deliver it to the world. Therefore, because of conviction, repentance, and confession every believer has a connection to Almighty God. Without Holy Spirit, the Body of Christ is rendered powerless.

5. *Conversion, or Transformation:* To change in character, or cause to turn from an evil life to a righteous one is *conversion*; it is a fundamental change brought about by Holy Spirit. In conversion, people are given a completely new heart which alters the mind, the heart, and the will. Therefore, salvation is called the "new birth." As new creations, believers are no longer children of Satan, they are now children of God.

Paul is challenging the Body of Christ to wake up and be filled with Holy Spirit. He is telling us to renew the mind we were given, prior to birth, in order to have a "right," biblical perspective. The bible never deviates from the instruction to "repent or turn away from sin." So, in order to convert the world, God expects us to repent, or change the way we think. Through the act of repentance, how people feel, process, and react will also change. Everything changes when people begin to think, and apply, right perspectives. *Philippians 2:5 states, "Let this mind be in you, which was also in Christ Jesus."* Religion sees repentance as the method used to stop sinning. This method is shallow and attached to the salvation experience and does not reflect the mind of Christ. As His mind is so shall our mind be. As the Body of Christ shifts to His way of thinking, the Kingdom of God gets brighter and brighter.

God's favor will occur as the Body of Christ stops being performance oriented and begins living by the Word of God. The modern-day Babel is conditioned to believe a pseudo-religion which compromises revelation for religious interpretation. As a result, people are living lies rather than truth; they are deceived and do not know it. Unfortunately, hypocrisy is rampant among this group of people. They say one thing and do the exact opposite. In addition to hypocrisy, church has succumbed to being about comfort, success, and feelings; it has become an all about "me" culture. Instead, the "true" church should be the most powerful entity on planet earth. *Oh God, have mercy on the Church. Help us to see through the darkness of religion and walk in the Light of Life.*

As the Church begins to hunger and thirst for righteousness, rather than the intoxicating feelings of a worldly system, they will be filled. When our minds are renewed to the purposes and plans of the Almighty, then our spheres of influence will begin changing to reflect His Kingdom. Those are the moments when heaven's door is opened, and the favor of God is revealed. At this point, true freedom is within the grasp of the Church.

STOP LIVING FOR GOD'S LOVE AND START LIVING FOR HIS FAVOR

Being Highly Favored is my desire; how about you? To achieve this position, the Church must not live like the world. We are told to seek His Kingdom first as well as His righteousness, then, all the things the Gentiles seek will be added unto us. Though the Church is not of this world, they are still in it and must work through the world's systems. However, their source is the Kingdom of God, not the world system. And, because the Church is connected to another place, our power comes in knowing our value. Therefore, our purpose is driven by value not by performance. So, it is important to avoid any attempts of fitting in, for, God has already accepted us. Begin to live out of His perception rather than dying out of wrong perception. Do not just do church, be the church. Live for the pleasure and purpose of the Kingdom. It is here that we attract God's divine favor.

Finding the Field of Favor

Chapter 2

Being Favored

In the sixth month, God sent the angel Gabriel to Nazareth, a town in Galilee, 27 to a virgin pledged to be married to a man named Joseph, a descendant of David. The virgin's name was Mary. 28 The angel went to her and said, "Greetings, you who are highly favored! The Lord is with you." (Luke 1:26-28 NIV)

And the angel came in unto her, and said, Hail, thou that art highly favored, the Lord is with thee: blessed art thou among women. **(Luke 1:28 KJV)**

As a young woman, Mary was chosen to be supernaturally impregnated with the seed of Almighty God. She was to call Him, Jesus, and He would be the Son of God. He is known as:

1. *The savior of humanity,*
2. *The King of the Universe,*
3. *The very image of God, and*
4. *The first born among many...*

In awe, I wonder, "How can this be? Why did God choose Mary? Why did God consider her to be *highly favored* among women?" The human mind is unable to comprehend how Holy Spirit could impregnant Mary without physical contact. However, God says that all things are possible to those that believe. Faith is the key. Mary trusted that God's Word would come to pass, then, she went through the process.

When God calls an individual to be impregnated with His Word, or His will, it is necessary to remember, *The Lord Your God is with you."* His purpose is always for the expansion of the Kingdom of God. Therefore, I often say, *"without God, man cannot, but without man, God will not."* Because God

24

stands by man, success is available for every assignment; this is Favor.

"What then shall we say to these things? If God is for us, who can be against us?" (Romans 8:31 NKJV)

When God extends His approval towards people, it is amazing that no enemy can steal His favor from them. The real power lies in our Father's desire to partner with His children. Again, "without His children, God will not." So, stop waiting on God and, instead, partner with Him for success. Like Mary, be impregnated, then carry, birth, and manage the seed of favor.

Please understand, God will not give people anything they are not able to manage. Though a person is praying for a specific thing, God will only give according to what he is equipped to handle. I suggest, first pray for the equipping, then receive what has been asked for. Manage the Word and the Promise will come. The blessing is hidden, within the darkness of the womb, waiting for the pressure that will deliver it into the world.

When God chose Mary, He had already favored her; He had already determined she could carry the weight of His seed. He also knew Joseph could manage the weight of His Word. Today, it is just as important to evaluate ourselves as to whether, or not, we are willing to carry His seed to term. Then, like Mary, birth it, manage its growth, while, at the same time, preparing to let it go. Mary and Joseph were willing. The question is, are we?

Once impregnated with God's seed, it will never be easy to carry. With Mary's submission, Holy Spirit overshadowed her to fill her womb with the promised Seed, the Son of God and the son of man. This was a huge burden to carry because it went against all the norms of her culture. It is good to keep in mind, "Favor attracts attack…before it attracts abundance." I am sure many questions flowed through Mary's mind regarding this pregnancy. One of which, "How do I explain this to my family and friends?" Another, "Will I be killed for an act of adultery that I did not commit? And *"Will Joseph divorce me?"* All these questions, and more, had to be left in God's hands because she had agreed to carry His seed. Obviously, Mary's ways were pleasing to the Lord, therefore, God would take care of her as well as His seed.

"When a man's ways please the LORD, He makes even his enemies to be at peace with him." (Proverbs 16:7 NKJV)

To experience the power of His resurrection, carrying His seed, or His favor, is a must. Mary's submission, to this extraordinary event, is a witness to all those who desire to give their all to the Lord. To carry His seed was a choice she could have rejected. However, she kept her eyes off the inconveniences, the hardships, and the challenges and kept her eyes on the Promise. It was the Promise that carried His seed to term, helped her through the delivery, and enabled her to experience the joy of His birth. Then, the Promise caused His seed to grow in wisdom, and stature, with God and man.

Father God, implant the seed of life into Your people. Holy Spirit, hover over us, as You did Mary, and fill our wombs with the breath of life. Equip us with the favor necessary to be carriers of the Word of God.

Mary's willingness proved, to God, that He could trust her with this assignment. My question is, "can God trust me to birth His assignment?" Mary was willing to carry this baby to term without knowing all the consequences; in those days, women were stoned to death for adultery. Her culture was not a forgiving one and, initially, Joseph wanted to, secretly, divorce her.

Unfortunately, people today do not seem to be as willing to give of themselves to fulfill the plans of God; this is especially true if a person's reputation is at stake. People are creatures of comfort so, when it rains, some stay home from church rather than attend services. Life is good if their plans and schedules come before kingdom. Most people want a god they can control; they want the golden calf. As a result, grace has been cheapened. And, under this cheap grace, it is too easy to say *"no"* when asked to give up something we love for the things that God loves. However, to walk in divine power, and favor, this cheap mindset must be renewed to Kingdom understanding. Thankfully, God revealed to us that Mary was "Highly Favored." She is an example for all to follow.

What is Favor?

Favor is God's endorsement. It is the state of being approved or held in high regard. In Luke 1:30, Gabriel was sent to tell Mary that she had found favor with God. As a result, nothing, the enemy tried, stopped what He sent Jesus to accomplish. Favor is also divine empowerment. He chose Mary and empowered her to accomplish His purposes; she would not have to walk through this assignment alone. All God needed from Mary and Joseph was a willingness to:

1. Receive by faith,
2. Lay down their present season in order to carry something greater,
3. Endure false accusations knowing that they are fulfilling God's purpose, and
4. Fight through for the good of others.

Can God Trust You? Can God Endorse you?

All people live in streams of favor. Those who are promoted, or successful, arrived there with the help of others; this is known as "common favor." This type of favor can happen just about anywhere: at school, on a sports team, on the playground, at work, etc. However, there is a type of favor that moves hell and unlocks divine power. This favor is known as "uncommon favor, or divine favor" It unlocks divine power at an accelerated force. It is an endorsement that comes from within the spirit of man; this power is much stronger than external pressures. So, common favor is an external favor that comes from man. And, uncommon favor comes from a deeper place, within man, which comes from God.

"The Kingdom is neither here or there, the kingdom is within you" (Luke 17:21)

Uncommon favor is a witness of the Almighty's hand upon a person's life. This opens the door for promotion, blessing, and protection. This type of favor empowers the individual with an internal peace, or calmness, which enables them to go through stressful situations without fear or worry. In this favor, there is power to combat any negative information attempting to sabotage the business, or life, of the individual. As an example, God did not place favor on Mary; however, He placed His favor within her. The uncommon favor she would be filled with was *the seed of God.* This favor would give her the peace necessary to see her through the storms that would, ultimately, come as a result of this pregnancy.

What did Mary do to warrant such high appreciation from Almighty God? Did He know she had a willing heart to go through an uncomfortable season? Did He know she would be willing to sacrifice everything to carry His favor? She made a tradeoff, the natural for the supernatural – she traded her life for His. There are many examples of this in the Bible including:

- Abraham was willing to sacrifice Isaac
- Joseph was thrown in a pit, captured, and sold into slavery; he was falsely accused and thrown into prison
- Noah built an ark
- Moses was removed from his family as a baby
- Samson was born a Nazirite, he could not cut his hair

Divine favor has a price tag; it always costs something. For some, fear will distract them from going through the wilderness for them to enter their promised land. However, when favor begins to produce fruit, they will move out of lack and into more than enough. It is encouraging to know that blessing is available to everyone God endorses.

"Now it shall come to pass, if you diligently obey the voice of the LORD your God, to observe carefully all His commandments which I command you today, that the LORD your God will set you high above all nations of the earth. And all these blessings shall come on thee, and overtake thee, if thou shalt hearken unto the voice of the LORD thy God. **(Deuteronomy 28:1,2 NKJV)**

Why Did God Choose Mary?

1. She came from Galilea, meaning expectation. God is attracted to expectation and wanted His seed raised in that atmosphere.
2. Mary was engaged to Joseph; and he was from the house of David who represented the house of praise. God

placed His seed within the genealogy of the House of Praise – which is the brick that builds the house of favor.

3. Regardless of her feelings, Mary would believe God. *"Blessed is she that believed: for there shall be a performance of those things, which had told her from the Lord." (Luke 1:45 NKJV)*

4. Mary understood that one day, she would have to give God's seed back to Him. Her responsibility was in raising His seed then sowing Him for the redemption of the world.

5. In Mary's culture, becoming pregnant outside of marriage created terrible accusations. However, God must have trusted that Mary would respond well to the opinions of others.

Jesus said to him, "If you can believe, all things are possible to him who believes." (Mark 9:23 NKJV)

Because Mary believed God, He was able to perform everything He had spoken regarding Jesus. Her belief system helped bring about the harvest of God's plan. To *believe* means to have confidence in the truth, the existence, or the reliability of something; although, without absolute proof that one is right in doing so. Faith, trust, acceptance, and conviction also describe belief.

It is important to understand, God is only as big, or powerful, as one believes. He is all-powerful, all-knowing, and He encompasses everything. God is not a man nor a created being. He is, and always will be, the Great I AM. However, unless a person's belief system can comprehend the vastness of God Himself, his believing will limit Him to what he can accept. Mary chose to take God at His word; therefore, God did everything He said.

Hesitation is Disobedience!

When a person vacillates between the word of God and his own desires, this is proof that God's instructions are not trusted. Hesitation communicates, to Him, the individual is not fully, convinced the instruction is worth obeying. It also reveals, what is wanted is greater than what is instructed.

"But let him ask in faith, with no doubting, for he who doubts is like a wave of the sea driven and tossed by the wind. For let not that man suppose that he will receive anything from the Lord; he is a double-minded man, unstable in all his ways. **(James 1:6-8 NKJV)**

Being a double-minded man, or a man that hesitates between two opinions, is weak. Hebrews 11:6 states, *"But without faith it is impossible to please Him, for he who comes to God must believe that He is, and that He is a rewarder of those who diligently seek Him."* Doubt does not please God and it strips the believer of receiving anything from Him. So, no longer hesitate between the Word of Holy Spirit and the word of flesh; the flesh will lie. Instead, listen and obey the instructions given from the God who knows all, the One who cannot lie.

7 Characteristics of a Double-Mind

1. Focused on **self-satisfaction** rather than pleasing God
2. Allow feelings and emotions to be the influence
3. Thoughts do not line up with the Word of God
4. Led by the Spirit except when self-interests get in the way

5. Void of the inner peace that comes with following God
6. Succumbs to old feelings and habits
7. Resists correction and direction

Favor is not for the double-minded, however, it is for those who act on the word of God without hesitation. When impressed by Holy Spirit to sow a seed, or help another person, it is good to act immediately. Otherwise, thoughts or questions could get in the way of obedience to His instruction. Then, the justifying begins, disobedience wins, and the opportunity to receive His blessing is lost. Being unstable disconnects the religious, or hesitant, mindset from His blessing. God wants to favor His people, but He will not favor those who are "wishy washy." So, be a person of faith who pleases God; He will favor the one who believes Him.

"Don't live for God's love, live for God's favor."
God calls those who act immediately, "Highly Favored."

To be *Highly Favored,* every person should act quickly on the Word of God, therefore, without hesitation. The willingness to respond quickly causes favor to flow. So, when God asks something of a person, He is endeavoring to release His blessing into the situation. And there is a proportionate harvest attached to every sown seed.

Favor is a Seed Before it is a Harvest
If people thought about Mary's extraordinary faith, they would realize God did everything He said He would do. Why? Because she believed Him. Her faith was at a level enabling God to miraculously conceive, then bring forth, His Son into the

earth. The Son of God, supernaturally, came into the earth through the womb of a woman. How incredible is that?

Double Favor

While I was sitting in my office, on a Friday afternoon, God directed me to go to a particular furniture store. He also requested I take the Youth Pastor along with the Praise and Worship Pastor – a married couple. I was in the middle of a project and did not want to be distracted. I was not able to leave and, on top of it, I did not need any furniture. Therefore, I did not want to go, and I began telling Holy Spirit I would go tomorrow. However, He said, "Go now!" So, in obedience, I took them to the furniture store.

Upon arriving, I immediately sensed I had made the right decision; I recognized the Lord had gone before us. Prior to today, I had heard the phrase, *"Money doesn't follow people, it's waiting on them."* That means, when a person is where they are supposed to be, the door of blessing is unlocked. When the store owner recognized me, her face lit up and she declared, "Bishop, I've been waiting on you to come back." She began telling me how their sales had doubled from the last time she had seen me. And then, she preceded to hand me a hundred-dollar bill. She had been keeping it in the cash register for the next time she saw me. Now, I understood why God chose this furniture store; He had a blessing waiting on me. Again, *"Money doesn't follow people, it's waiting on them."* Thankfully, God knows where the blessings are and, if we are obedient, we will receive the favor He has scheduled for us.

While I was receiving the store owner's seed money, the Praise and Worship Pastor had been admiring a beautiful statue. So, the owner asked her, "Do you like this statue?" The response was, "Oh, I do!" Upon hearing her response, the statue was given to her. Remember, God instructed me to bring both the Praise and Worship Pastor as well as the Youth Pastor. Because I obeyed His instruction, "to go," they experienced God's favor as well. I walked out of that store a hundred dollars richer and they had a beautiful statue for their home. God gave me access to His instruction and they had access to me which enabled them to receive the overflow of favor. Connections are powerful blessings.

As we were driving back to the office, Holy Spirit said, *"How would you like to know where money, favor, and blessing is every single day? Money, or blessing, is not following you, it is waiting on you. I can show you where your blessings are every single day. All you must do is labor to hear my voice."* **This applies to everyone.** God wants everyone to receive what He has for them. God desires favor to be active in every believer. He is not a respecter of persons; when He favors one, He favors ALL. The only requirements are to hear then obey His instructions.

"Believe it, receive it… Doubt it, do without it!"

Now is the time to shout, "I AM READY FOR A LIFE OF FAVOR!

Chapter 3

The Key
To
Favor is Access

Finding the Field of Favor

*Without favor, there is no success but, with favor, there is
access. Favor will change and will schedule seasons while
faith decides favor's timing.*

In preparation for a new season, God will provide access
through individuals willing to allow people into their world. A
true mentor desires teaching their ways, of success, to motivated,
self-driven people. Mentorship is success without all the pain.
It is life without mistakes and decisions without failure. Access
is a powerful gift granted by favor; it can bring acceleration to
success. Favor can place entrepreneurs in a room with great
people for us to hear the conversations of the successful and the
wealthy.

Access is a powerful key to a life not fought, or paid, for.
It grants opportunity to learn while enabling an individual to take
hold of a lifestyle that, at one time, was only a dream: one far
from reach. Favor is access!

Steps to Favor

Be One Who Stands Out

When Boaz noticed Ruth gleaning in his barley fields,
Ruth's life began to change. Boaz recognized her as the
daughter-in-law of Naomi and preceded to endorse her with his
favor. Boaz said to Ruth, **"*You will listen, my daughter, will you
not? Do not go to glean in another field, nor go from here, but
stay close by my young women. Let your eyes be on the field
which they reap and go after them. Have I not commanded the
young men not to touch you? And when you are thirsty, go to
the vessels and drink from what the young men have drawn."
(Ruth 2:8-9 NKJV)* He** also commanded his young men, **"*Let
her glean even among the sheaves, and do not reproach her.***

Also let grain from the bundles fall purposely for her; leave it that she may glean, and do not rebuke her." (Ruth 2:15-16 NKJV)

While living in the land of Moab, Ruth's husband died. And, as it turned out, so did her father-in-law and brother-in-law. Because there was a famine in Moab, Naomi made the decision to return to Judah where God was giving His people bread. Then, after Ruth saw the wisdom in Naomi's decision, she continued the journey with her. Unfortunately, it is from a feeling, rather than wisdom, that some people seek to connect to a mentor; this is attachment for acceptance, not connection. A leach will attach to a blood source until the life is sucked out of it, then, it will detach in order to find another source. Attachment seeks after a feeling and a handout while connection seeks information regarding the mentor's life, their experiences, along with their wisdom. One is attached to a moment while the other is connected to a future. Qualified mentors will know the difference.

Unknowingly, Ruth connected herself to Naomi, her mentor, who would link her to her future. Ruth made the decision to make Naomi's God, her God, therefore, her connection was to a life of favor rather than a temporary feeling. Through Naomi's mentorship, Ruth was strategically placed in a position to be noticed by Boaz. The right mentors will always do this so, it is important to, stop living for a moment, or a feeling, and live for a great future. Being noticed, or liked, by everyone is not necessary, but the right mentor is. In Ruth's day there were many landowners, with many fields to glean in, however, she obeyed Naomi, her mentor, and went to Boaz's field.

As a result of Ruth's obedience, Boaz favored her more than anyone else in the field. He commanded extra grain be left for her as well as protection from the young men. Favor increased her and will always increase those who walk in His favor.

The Jonathan Connection

After David killed Goliath, he was given immediate access to Saul's throne. The throne gave him access to the palace which then gave him access to Jonathan, Saul's son. This connection would be needed for David to maintain his access to the throne; and, staying connected is the real sign of favor. It was necessary for David to make his presence known as well as to stay in that kingly environment to learn and grow. There would be no point in him being in the palace if he could not make a difference. So, God placed Jonathan in David's life to befriend him, teach him, and help him get to his next season. It was an unlikely friendship due to the fact, "It was Saul's son, who was in line for the throne." However, Jonathan was the one who protected, and even promoted, David whom God had chosen to replace Saul, as King. Their friendship was a picture of true covenant and love. It was Jonathan who taught David Kingdom protocol and etiquette. And it was Jonathan who taught David Kingdom posture and manners. *Remember, favor is access.*

Access

Access is defined as the approach or entry of a place; it is the way in. In this place, God speaks to the person who will become the mentor for someone's next season. To trivialize access is disastrous, so treat it with respect. Right presentation is necessary as well. Take the time to study the ways, posture, and dress of those in whom mentorship is being sought. This is what Joseph did when he found himself a slave to the Pharoah of Egypt. He learned their practices and mannerisms and, though it was not Israelite custom, he shaved his beard and cut his hair prior to gaining access to Pharoah. He also dressed appropriately in honor of Pharoah's status. It is important to understand, those who give access discern the ones who are favored. For favor will determine whether the mentor will give of his time, or energy, into helping others understand palace protocol.

People Must Be Noticed

According to Mike Murdock, "the Law of Recognition teaches, *"Everything you need, in your life, is already in your life; it is merely awaiting your recognition of it."* In a restaurant, many years ago, a Man of God approached me while I was standing at the salad bar. He spoke these words, *"The question is, Not, are you? but, when are you?"* The question is not, "am I chosen or is the hand of greatness on me." The question is not, "am I going to be wealthy or am I going to be great." However, the question is, *"when* am I going to be wealthy? *When* am I going to be great?" This refers to His timing. In time, people struggle to make things happen; however, it is in the struggle people learn how to be, and act, in His timing. Time prepares them for the manifestation of the blessing.

The Man of God, whose ministry and life tripled mine, discerned the hand of favor on my life and decided to help me make the connection into my next season. The Law of Favor helps people who are full of desire, talent, skill, and ability with the mentorship that enables them to succeed. Favor recognizes and promotes, it teaches and instructs, and it moves people into their destiny. For this to take place, God's endorsement is needed. Then, everything that was held back is released. May the power of endorsement open the door for people to enter their next season.

Discern Those Who Notice

Unfortunately, it is not enough to be recognized, or noticed, but it is necessary to discern a divine moment; an encounter with those who have been favored by God. In this moment, it is important to keep composure. Maintain a self-controlled state of mind by refraining from talking about, "ME." Instead, determine to sow, or pour, honor into their lives. Remember, it is important to gain their mentorship rather than their support. They are there to teach knowledge and wisdom; leave their money alone. And, if receiving of their wealth is the motivation, favor will be terminated. He is not your source, God is every man's source, every man's financial benefactor. Working the law of Honor will bring accelerated growth to those who practice it.

Being a Servant is Key

Being a servant involves identifying, or anticipating, problems and then, removing, or solving them. People who serve in ministry not only help the Minister, but are also servants, of God, in that ministry. Unfortunately, most people are unwilling to give of themselves to support their Church; they have not understood the law of servanthood. They visit, get born-again, are excited to learn the Word, then disappear after, maybe, five-years. Instead of truly plugging in, they allowed schedules and activities to pull them away. Their only connection was in attending Church services; but they neglected the Body. And those who get paid for their services are not servants, they are employees. So, when the minister starts asking people to step into serving positions, answer the call. There are many opportunities to serve: parking lot duty, nursery helpers, youth teachers and volunteers, cleaning team, musicians and singers, media helpers, landscape workers, prayer teams, altar workers, maintenance crew, follow-up teams, etc. Remember, serving is, "loving others as you love yourself."

How should people respond when a need is presented?

Serving is an act of honor, not only towards the Minister, but to God. Proverbs 3:27 states, *"Do not withhold good from those whom it is due, when it is in the power of your hand to do so." (NKJV)* Honor is good and should be given to the Man of God; especially to those who, truly, imitate Christ and teach Kingdom authority. Anything less is disobedience. And, while serving in ministry, all focus should be on the Lord; for, *"It is the Lord Christ you are serving." (Colossians 3:24 NIV)* So, I encourage all believers, be the extension of God's hand and serve His people.

Ask Questions Before Serving

1. *What needs to be done?* Make observations, then ask questions. What can I do to help serve God's purpose? What can I do to make a difference?

2. *Am I able to solve this problem?* Even though someone may see a problem, it does not mean they are the one who can meet that need. In God's house, He is the one who empowers people to help solve problems.

3. *Will I be able to serve with excellence?* Serving anything half-hearted is a bad idea. One, it makes people look useless and, two, it is a bad witness to those who are watching.

41

Two ways to be a servant include: listening to and supporting, the team. Listening is necessary in order to serve well; it is not for correcting. And, to make life easier, do not serve according to a preconceived timeline. As an example, for fifteen years, Elisha served Elijah by seeing that his needs were met; in other words, he took care of the prophet. According to 2 Kings 3:11, Elisha even *"poured water on the hands of Elijah."* *(NKJV)* Throughout the time he served Elijah, Elisha was watering the seeds of his destiny which had been locked up in the prophet. He served him until the transfer of anointing took place. *"He also took up the mantle of Elijah that had fallen from him." (2 Kings 2:13 NKJV)* Elisha stayed with Elijah until he saw him no more because God had taken him. Elijah was not blind to who was following him, therefore, Elisha's persistence enabled God's favor to manifest through the receiving of his mantle. This is an incredible, powerful truth.

Unpopular Counsel

I was at the Winter Wisdom Conference, in Dallas, and had just finished preaching. As I was approaching my product table, a man came to me asking how he could get into the ministry. Unfortunately, my response was not what he wanted to hear. I informed him that it would be necessary for him to get plugged into a church and start serving. I also told him to find a man, or woman, of God that is able, and willing, to be a mentor because not all have that ability. A mentor is called to be a father, or a mother, to their spiritual sons and daughters.

"There are many teachers but not many fathers. For though you might have ten thousand instructors in Christ, yet you do not have many fathers; for in Christ Jesus, I have begotten you through the gospel." (I Cor 4:15 NKJV)

I told him, *"Once you find a mentor, join that church, then start serving him."* Because it was not what he wanted to hear, he became angry. Then, he condescendingly replied, *"SERVE A MAN OF GOD?"* My reply, *"ABSOLUTELY!"* Serving a man of God can include: 1) ensuring he is prepared with everything necessary for ministering; 2) making sure his accommodations are comfortable; 3) running errands for him; 4) supplying water, mints, or snacks; 5) being aware of his needs and meeting them; and 6) praying for him. Basically, serving him makes his life, as a minister easier, or better. Due to the young man's response, it was obvious he was not receiving the mentorship. He stated, *"I am called to preach. I am called to win the nations. God has called me to do great things. Servanthood is not doing great things."* However, I disagree!

But he who is greatest among you shall be your servant. (Matt 23:11 NKJV)

To do great things requires every person to be a servant to God. In Psalms 133 it states, *"How good and how pleasant it is for brothers to live together in unity."* Unity is like **"OIL"** that flows down from Aaron's head to his beard and then, to his clothes. (Paraphrased) It is not possible for oil to flow up; it always flows down. In this verse, the oil is flowing down from his head to his beard, then to his garments. The oil, or the anointing, does not start in a seat, it starts in the high mountain of the Lord, then flows down toward those called, by Him, to serve in training. Where is it flowing? It is flowing on then through the body. It starts at the head then flows through leadership; however, its focus is the garment. The law of gravity causes the oil to gather at the lowest parts, of the garment, where it begins to puddle. This is where people show up, on their own time, to clean and take care of the ministry. The oil travels toward the servant; the law of soaking power and favor is attracted to serving.

Facts of Servanthood

1. The anointing people serve will, most likely, be the anointing they carry.
2. Learning to serve correctly takes time.
3. If people feel as if no one recognizes their serving, remember, "God is watching."
4. The transfer of favor is on the people who serve.
5. Servanthood is the proof people have stopped loving their own interests and have begun to love God's instead.
6. By example, Jesus taught how to be a servant (Matthew 10:24)
7. Servanthood is a golden key to unlocking the door of promotion.
8. Great leaders have always been uncommon servants. Joshua served Moses; Esther served the king; Jonathan served David; Elisha served Elijah; David served Saul; Ruth served Naomi; and, Joseph served in prison as well as in the palace. Every place he served he was promoted to the top levels of authority.
9. A servant is pursued by great leaders.
10. The uncommon servant always prospers.

God calls people for the purpose of serving others. Therefore, it is necessary to make a determined effort to do so with all diligence and excellence.

Divine Timing

To close, let me add this thought. Do not promote yourself, keep serving. Be patient! Wait on Godly timing. As you are serving, God is moving. Remember, waiters are winners. Be comfortable with His timing. God has set an appointed time, I promise! Your scheduled encounter is coming; it has already been written down in God's appointment book. He has not forgotten you. It is very important to understand, it is necessary to wait on God to promote you; for, whatever promotes must be able to sustain as well. If a person self-promotes himself, then that person must have the ability to also sustain himself when trouble shows up. Whoever is doing the elevating must have the resources available to sustain the person in crisis. The elevator must have the ability to sustain, strengthen, and support that person physically, emotionally, and mentally. They must have the power to comfort, help, assist, encourage, and to support. However, God is the only One, the only Source who has the power, ability, and wisdom to do all those things. *Self has no ability or power to hold you in troubled times.* In order to be favored, you must wait on divine times; and God must be the one who promotes.

Finding the Field of Favor

Chapter 4

The Essence
of
Favor

Now a certain man was there who had an infirmity thirty-eight years. (John 5:5 NKJV)

Fragrance is defined as a *pleasant and sweet smell*. It can be a strong, atmosphere changer. Walking into a restaurant with freshly brewed coffee, or waking up to that wonderful aroma, can move someone who dislikes coffee to wishing they had some. Like freshly, popped popcorn, or fried chicken, certain smells attract people's senses. And, by pumping those irresistible smells into the atmosphere, businesses understand they can produce more sells for their company.

There are also certain smells, fragrances, or aromas that can bring to remembrance an old memory. This happens to me when I smell my wife's perfume; it floods my heart with fresh, new emotions for her. As one of five major senses in the human body, smell is as powerful as seeing. To me, cologne is an addiction, therefore, I put it on every day; and I own a variety of brands. My wife will ask, "Why do you wear cologne to cut the grass?" Because I like the way cologne smells, *"It is in my power to decide what I smell not the environment around me."*

It is hard to imagine how the mind can differentiate between all the smells wafting through the air. There are thousands, if not millions, or trillions of odors the mind is able to detect. And they enable the mind to recreate past feelings, or emotions such as love, joy, and grief; these scents are attached to memories, good or bad. God created the sense of smell because He Himself knows the value of scent. 2 Corinthians 2:15 states, *"For we are to God the fragrance of Christ among those who are being saved and among those who are perishing."* *(NKJV)* Fragrance matters! It is interesting that, while God expects people to master their feelings and emotions, He uses the sense of smell to reveal what needs to be mastered. According to "The Aroma of the Knowledge of God: How the

Sense of Smell Inspires Worship and Awe" by Aaron Sathyanesan, there are three broad patterns regarding the sense of smell in Scripture:

- **God Can Smell Too**

  Most people think of the God, of the Bible, as One who watches over them, however there is scriptural evidence that supports how His sense of smell keeps track of them as well. In Genesis, following the flood, when Noah comes out of the Ark, he made burnt offering sacrifices on the altar. Afterwards, we are told, God smelled the aroma of that sacrifice and it moved Him to declare He would never again curse the ground because of humans. Noah's altar created a fragrance that attracted God's favor thereby releasing His mercy upon the land.

  "The Lord smelled the pleasing aroma and said in his heart: "Never again will I curse the ground because of humans, even though every inclination of the human heart is evil from childhood. And never again will I destroy all living creatures, as I have done." (Genesis 8:21 NKJV)

- **God Related Smell to Purity**

  According to this article, there is a connection between the sense of smell and the purification laws of ancient Israel. Smells could be associated with what was perceived as "clean versus unclean, or holy versus unholy." At that time, "clean" determined the boundaries, or limits, of life versus death; or, the blessing versus the curse. The story of Lazarus gives a better understanding of the boundaries established between the smell of life and the smell of death. At Jesus' command, *"take away the stone,"* Martha warned Him, *"Lord, by this time there is a stench, for he has been dead four days."* (John 11:39 NKJV)

- **Smell is Mysterious**

   Smell is mysterious in that the object creating the odor is not always apparent; the wind could be carrying the aroma far from its source. It is not limited to its place of origin, nor time, because it can drift until the smell dissipates. In the Old Testament, the Hebrew word for "spirit" is Ruach. According to the <u>International Standard Bible Encyclopedia,</u> the verb form of Ruach means, literally, to breathe, to inhale, thence to smell. So, in the beginning, God made a connection between the spirit and with the ability to smell.

And the Lord God formed man of the dust of the ground and breathed into his nostrils the breath of life; and man became a living being. **(Genesis 2:7 NKJV)**

There is a Powerful Mystery in Aroma

   At first glance, the fifth chapter of the book of John, describes a vast number of sick people laying throughout the five-porches of the Bethesda pool, or "house of mercy." They were there waiting for a miracle that would heal them. As horrible as the waiting must have been, what filled the atmosphere was bad too. It was permeated with their moaning and crying as well as the stench of sickness and disease. Then, Jesus - the Healer, the King of kings, and the Lord of lords –

walks up to a man who had been sick for thirty-eight years. He had to move through a tremendous crowd to find the one God had previously shown Him. Nevertheless, Jesus found him waiting for an angel to stir the waters; the stirring was a sign indicating the waters were ready and someone would be healed. However, when the stirring of the water began, he would be required to enter the water first to be healed.

Now there is in Jerusalem by the Sheep Gate a pool, which is called in Hebrew, Bethesda, having five porches. 3) In these lay a great multitude of sick people, blind, lame, paralyzed, waiting for the moving of the water. 4) For an angel went down at a certain time into the pool and stirred up the water; then whoever stepped in first, after the stirring of the water, was made well of whatever disease he had. 5) Now a certain man was there who had an infirmity thirty-eight years. (John 5:2-4 NKJV)

Chapter five shows a great multitude of needy, hurting people and reveals the sick as blind, lame, and paralyzed; and it implies that Jesus walked past them all. Though He is the Healer, and He has the power to solve every need, He does not stop. He is focused! It seems odd that Jesus did not do anything to help the suffering of this crowd. He saw their needs, saw they were hurting, and even heard their cries, yet does nothing. *Jesus shows them no favor!* Because of this, it is important to do away with the myth, *"God is only interested in the crowd; He is only moved by their needs."* This myth is not true because He walked by the whole crowd to get to one man.

6) When Jesus saw him lying there, and knew that he already had been in that condition a long time, He said to him, "Do you want to be made well?" 7) The sick man answered Him,

"Sir, I have no man to put me into the pool when the water is stirred up; but while I am coming, another steps down before me." **(John 5:5-7 NKJV)**

God is Not Moved by Need; He is Moved by Essence!

Essence is defined as the inward nature, or true substance of a thing. The first time I heard this statement, I felt a bit angry. Why isn't God moved by our need? And, if God was moved by need, why didn't Jesus heal those who had gathered around the Bethesda pool? Because need does not attract Him. Nevertheless, people's needs are important, but God moves according to a different plan. *"He is not a man"* who is led by feelings or emotions. Again, Jesus walked by all the other sick men, women, and children. He did this to find the, one, man who had had an infirmity for thirty-eight years. He was attracted to his persistence not the miracle he apparently needed. Thirty-eight-years equals thirteen thousand, three hundred and eighty days of going to that pool. The essence, or inward nature, of this man was one of persistence.

Every single day, he fought the same struggles, yet he persistently followed the same routine. And, every day, he went home broken, feeble, and weak; he was bound by his infirmity. What motivated him to continue this, seemingly, futile endeavor? Did his family and friends discourage this activity with questions and comments of their own? Did his neighbors criticize and demean his determination? The disappointment had to have been unbearable but, somehow, he pushed through and clung to the hope that kept driving him to that pool. He did not choose a porch, he chose hope. The Lord once said to me, *"Endurance is a qualifier."* So, for this man, at the end of those long thirty-eight years, the reward for believing, pursuing, and enduring was recovery of everything lost. His formula for divine encounters included: 1) endure through the pain, failure, and loss; 2) never stop pursuing the miracle; 3) believe in the future without focusing on the past; and, 4) loss is the seed for divine recovery.

God Will Respond When People Begin Reaching

Not only did his persistence attract God's favor, but his pursuit did as well. The man pursued God, and the miracle he needed, for thirty-eight years. He did not give up or quit. He did not lose focus but continued in his pursuit until Jesus came to him. If his goal included waiting on something to happen, he would have died in his infirmity. However, he made the decision to pursue, stay in expectation, continue to believe, and then endure until the end. This attitude seems to parallel with the idea behind the unnamed porch which was empty of people. Unfortunately, while amid failure and weakness, most of the people chose to "sit and wait." This group was not living, nor was it prospering; only existing. They are the ones who represent the other four porches.

Even though the crowds were a daily event, they only came to wait. As a result, due to the losses these people have endured, there was no longer any expectation or hope for healing. So, what were they waiting on? When the waters began to stir, did they fight to get to the water? Or, because of hopelessness, do nothing? Hopeless people become paralyzed and are unable to move forward. The Bible states that faith without works is dead so, it is possible, lack of effort killed their belief for healing. Faith is not wishing, and neither is hope. However, faith involves action and hope is confidence in a better outcome. Doing nothing, or waiting around until something happens, is not an option when people can use their faith.

Unfortunately, the world is full of people who believe that waiting around will work for their betterment. There are people who do nothing until they receive a prophetic word. They are waiting to be healed, waiting on a word, waiting to be noticed, waiting on a feeling, just waiting. The whole world seems to be waiting on a miracle. For this reason, it is important to understand, the people who limit themselves to a waiting mentality can attract God's love but they will not attract the favor of God.

God is love; therefore, He loves all the time. And, because that is who He is, striving for love is not necessary. As an example of loving people, He sent Jesus to the world to redeem them from a system they could not escape. Love is the game changer. And, according to 1 Corinthians 13:8, *"Love (God) never fails."* Love gives people the opportunity to change but He does not force change on anyone. Nevertheless, Holy Spirit teaches people to activate love for the purpose of walking in forgiveness toward those who hurt them, lied to them, or betrayed them. Loving my children has not changed them; however, it has helped me to stay in a position of, continuously, believing in them. My favor, on the other hand, is released to them when they do what is for their own good and betterment. When I can see them taking responsibility for themselves, their spouses, as well as their children, I am motivated to extend favor to them. Good, or bad, they have my love, but my favor is on a different level.

So, as much as people would love to see their miracle, it is imperative they also take responsibility for their lives without allowing the waiting to derail them. For thirty-eight years, the man of Bethesda went to the pool, and back, without neglecting his responsibilities; his wife, children, home, etc.

Desire and Action are Different

There is a huge difference between "wanting to" and "willing to." Most people have an "I want" mentality. So, rather than taking the initiative to obtain what is wanted, they do nothing. Miracles are not attracted by the need for one but by one's willingness to obtain it. The concept, "If a man does not work, he will not eat," applies here as well. For, every step a man takes moves his desire into reality. The energy of divine favor is released through the actions taken during times of need.

"For an angel went down at a certain season into the pool and troubled the water: whosoever then first after the troubling of the water stepped in was made whole of whatsoever disease he had." **(John 5:4 NKJV)**

The Bethesda man was seeking a daily encounter for his need, not yesterday's stirring. He intently stayed focused on his purpose for being at the pool rather than the failures of the past.

Seasons are Always Happening

According to John 5:4, *"the waters were stirred at a certain season."* And, in Ecclesiastes 3:1 it states, *"To everything there is a season."* There is a time to live, a time to die, a time to sow, a time to harvest, etc. The word season and time are interconnected and mean a period, of time. Time is always progressive; it always moves forward and will never move backwards. Time is in pursuit of "timing," therefore timing is future while time is current. Everything done in current circumstances, or time, will decide what God will do in the future, or timing.

It is important to know the seasons and the times, so people are always asking, "What time is it?" I say, "It is time for miracles, time for change, time to be favored, time for turnaround, and time to start looking to the future and forgetting the past."

There is a Season of Disruption Happening

Disruption is defined as *the act or process of disrupting something: a break or interruption in the normal course or continuation of some activity, or process.* It is in the seasons of disruption that God's favor is necessary. His favor is capable of disrupting and dismantling every strategy of the enemy; his plans have no power over the favor God extends. It is, now, the time to prepare for His divine interruption into everything the enemy has meant for evil.

Unfortunately, it is nearly impossible to avoid, or stop, a bad season once it starts. So, learning how to maneuver through those times is important. Thriving will be a challenge, but surviving is the goal. And the power to win is decided by the willingness to outlast, outlive, and survive in order to thrive in any season. It is also necessary to continue with forward momentum. Do not stop moving. Do not sit around waiting for change to happen, keep pursuing it; for progress and increase are determined by the decisions made during a delayed season. It has been said, "In order to win, you need a great defense." However, a great offense is needed as well. At times, it will be necessary to stop defending a season and, instead, attack it. The Bethesda man kept coming; he never gave up and God favored him with his next season. Fight for every opportunity to gain momentum and to resist giving up. Waiting for the right thing to happen is for those who have already given up. So, get up, get going, get involved, and persevere!

Favor Without Works is Welfare

Let me just say, God is not a proponent of welfare. Poverty becomes a prison when, instead of working, people want to be bailed out of their problems. God has given man the power that makes wealth as well as gifts and talents for him to have success in life. On the other hand, hell is determined to squelch all of that for man to live, dependently, off another. This is exactly what happened with the Israelites when they were made slaves in Egypt. (Read Genesis, chapter 40, and the whole book of Exodus)

Being Favored and "Doing a Favor" are Vastly Different

To be favored, by God, means that person has gained approval, acceptance, or special benefits or blessings. (Baker's Evangelical Dictionary of Biblical Theology) It means to validate, authorize, affirm, or mark with distinction. So, it is important to know the difference between favored or to be granted a favor. Remember, God is not the God of doing favors, instead, He is the God of Favor. According to "Dictionary.com," favor is defined as something done, or granted, out of goodwill; this is "doing a favor." Favor, on the other hand, is God's endorsement; it binds Him to the releasing of heaven's resources over the divine plan for a person's life. This is the same as having a signed contract with the kingdom of God. Jesus taught the disciples, *"Your kingdom come. Your will be done on earth as it is in heaven."* (Matthew 6:10 NKJV) He gave them a great contractual example believers have with the kingdom of God. It is time for the church to take up the mantle of walking in this realm of powerful, Kingdom Favor.

Because favor is God's divine endorsement, it opens the door for heaven's support and allows for the defense of His people; He will partner with them for their preservation. He will also ratify, confirm, and approve believers to the kingdom of darkness. *"And the evil spirit answered and said, 'Jesus I know, and Paul I know; but who are you?'"* (Acts 19:15 NKJV) Hell knows who God has approved. My question is, "who wouldn't want to give up their self-centered lifestyle in order to live in the favor of God?"

Doing someone a favor, on the other hand, is reflected in this statement, "If you do me a favor, I will do you a favor in return." This is not how God operates; He gives Favor. Many Pastors, in the past, have come to me stating, "you can preach at my church, if I can preach at yours." However, I refuse to allow a Pastor to speak at ChurchOne80 based on the return of a favor. It is preferrable to speak at churches who recognize God's anointing rather than being asked to do so with conditions. If the Pastor is not able to see how, through Holy Spirit, the congregation could go to a higher level of power, I would rather not be invited. Sadly, in most cases, favors come with strings attached. However, when God extends His Favor, He has already qualified that individual without strings attached. He gives Favor to those willing to do what is necessary to advance the Kingdom of God on earth.

It is time to get up…do something…move! Jesus will meet you at the point of your miracle. Give thanks, praise, worship, and study until the water is stirred, then, get in. Most importantly, do not get caught complaining during the waiting period; it could cost you your miracle.

Has Anyone Noticed?

Being at the right place, at the right time, is key to having the door of favor unlocked; otherwise, being noticed, by the right person, might not happen. John 5:6 states, *"When Jesus saw him lying there, and knew that he already had been in that condition a long time, He said to him, 'Do you want to be made well?'"* (NKJV) How did Jesus know to look for this man? It is probable, someone told him about his thirty-eight-year history of traveling to Bethesda. This man's consistency got Jesus' attention. I often wonder, how many people missed out on their miracle because the key of "consistency" was not applied? In my years of ministry, I have seen lots of people who began standing, in faith, for God's favor, but for lack of consistency, failed to receive it. They faithfully began attending church services, then, for various reasons, attendance dropped until they no longer showed up. Often, years later, I discovered they continued believing for His favor but, unfortunately, had not changed regarding their attendance. Failing in consistency kept them from the "Jesus" encounter they had desired.

Due to a lack of understanding regarding church attendance, the enemy was able to interrupt their encounter. If Jesus shows up during the stirring of the waters, what happens when the people are not there? Due to circumstances, or desires, pulling them away from church, the opportunity for favor was missed. And, instead of staying planted, they got impatient and began visiting a multitude of additional churches. Remember, the man of Bethesda was planted, in one place, for thirty-eight-years; he continued until he received the healing he was after. However, many today are easily offended and leave the house of their miracle.

The man of Bethesda was different in that, no matter his circumstances, he kept "attending" the waters. He was consistent with his attendance, he never gave up, and he continued seeking until Jesus found him at the pool. I am sure this thought kept him going, "if I don't get close enough to the pool, no one will help me get in when the waters begin to stir." It is sad to say, but there are lots of people who will not help others reach their goals; especially if they are at the same level of need. Human nature is naturally self-absorbed; it breeds selfishness, and it will look out for self. Unfortunately, to the other sick people, it did not matter that the Bethesda man had been there for thirty-eight-years. Why? Because they were all there for the same reason, healing. Thus, he had to keep pushing himself, otherwise, the waiting could go on indefinitely. He made the decision to show up until someone noticed. Consider the saying, "Nothing into Nothing Equals Nothing!" A seed must be sown to reap a harvest. His attendance reaped the harvest of healing along with everything lost during those thirty-eight, long, years. As a side note, in verse five, of John chapter five, the man of Bethesda was known as, *"a certain man."* Here, the Word of God is giving people the opportunity to apply their own name as well as their own needs. In other words, this phrase could apply to anyone or any need.

In this story, access opened the door for a sick man to receive healing, recovery, and restoration. After consistently going to the pool, one day he found himself in the right place at the right time for a miracle. In this arena, God sent Jesus who gave him the access needed to move forward, or for increase.

My prayer: Holy Spirit, reveal the path and access necessary for miracles and promotions to take place.

Jesus said to him, "Rise, take up your bed and walk." 9) And immediately the man was made well, took up his bed, and walked. And that day was the Sabbath. 10) The Jews therefore said to him who was cured, "It is the Sabbath; it is not lawful for you to carry your bed." 11) He answered them, "He who made me well said to me, 'Take up your bed and walk.'" 12) Then they asked him, "Who is the Man who said to you, 'Take up your bed and walk.'" **(John 5:8-12 KJV)**

Avoid the Porches

The pool of Bethesda was surrounded by five porches, four of which were not named. What was their purpose? And why wasn't the fifth one named? As Jesus was moving towards the "Bethesda man," he passed four of those porches which contained sick and needy people. They were also in need of Him; so, why didn't He stop? Was their present situation locking them out of their future? What happens when sick people get together? They talk about their infirmities, their pains, and their misfortunes. They tend to reflect on how those things have limited them in life and, as a result, they have become stuck. Their lives are empty and without direction.

Who Was on the Four Porches?

1. *The impotent* are those who lack power or ability to produce any significant or desired effect. They are powerless, unsuccessful, crippled, unproductive, fruitless, helpless, ineffective, inefficient, unfit, paralyzed, and hopeless. Powerlessness produces helplessness; there are a lot of these stories in the Bible.

   There are impotent people throughout our churches, homes, and society. They are limited in their working knowledge, so they have no strategy capable of setting themselves free. Unfortunately, they live day-to-day and from paycheck-to-paycheck without a clue as to how to go beyond what is easy. Some are bound by laziness, while others withhold what rightly belongs to God. Yet, others become takers and receivers rather than learning the art of giving. Even their work habits reflect how little they understand of God's principles. At this pace, they will never make a good impact on society. It should not be this way in the Kingdom of God. Nevertheless, there are impotent, powerless, and ineffective people with wrong perspectives producing very little for our King. Without a thought, this group will come to church to sing praises, worship, and listen to the message without serving in any capacity. Most of them will not get involved, neither will they fellowship, however, before leaving for another church, they will take all they can. Then, they vanish without saying a word.

2. *The Blind,* per the Greek definition, are those who are not able, or willing, to notice, understand, or judge correctly. This does not reflect physical blindness but mental. They are unwilling to see, or discern, the truth in order to change. As a result, most will begin judging, questioning, and criticizing those in leadership. Because of this, they are unable to see the greatness in others; instead, they are focused on the weaknesses of the leaders as well as the organization. Then, instead of keeping it to themselves, they begin exposing those things to everyone.

   Dangerous people spread the weaknesses of others and can destroy the vision of the leader in a matter of days. Their criticism is as the venom of a snake that goes throughout the whole body. And, before the bite wound is discovered, half the organization has been infected.

   Blind people do not lack the ability to change, however, they believe the other person should be the one that changes, not them. Because they are not "willing" to change, they are skilled roadblocks to any successful endeavor. Many times, I say, *"Demons don't destroy churches, people do."* However, with God's weapons, spiritually blind people can be stopped from destroying what others are building.

3. *Halted,* in the Greek, means to be uncertain, to waver, or to hesitate which is *disobedience.* Unfortunately, to be able to hear God's voice, and understand what He is saying, is pointless without being obedient. There have been multiple times, in the past, when I hesitated to obey His instructions; as a result, I missed out on His blessings. Because most people are not familiar with God's voice, it is easy to miss. It is not because people do not want to hear His voice, but they do not understand His ways. Not knowing how to really pray could be why some do not have a continuous dialog with the Father. And there are many things that can impede a person's conversation with God, including: limiting our prayers to only our problems and telling Him how to perform His will. However, very few people take the time to wait, in His presence, for Him to speak. If people were patient, God would use those opportunities to teach or give instructions. However, in most cases, hesitation is the very thing stopping His favor from flowing. For those who do wait in His presence, I encourage you to act swiftly at the hearing of His voice. As an example, a person's carnal nature will never prompt that individual into giving an offering for the advancement of the Kingdom of God, neither will Satan. So, upon hearing an instruction to give, do not hesitate. Remember, when giving, *"If your giving does not move you, it probably won't move God either."*

Give, and it will be given to you. A good measure, pressed down, shaken together, and running over, will be poured into your lap. For with the measure you use, it will be measured to you." (Luke 6:38 NIV)

4. *Withered,* in the Greek, means to lose vigor, or freshness. After being saved for a while, I have noticed many Christians seem miserable. They avoid worship service, and they hardly ever have a smile on their face. At one time, they seemed happy, but their problems found no solutions. Therefore, the Word is set aside while they focus on how long they have been coming to church instead. Discouragement has caused them to wither away in their giving, witness, joy, and love. The vigor they once had is gone along with the fresh fragrance of salvation.

I pray God give everyone who is impotent, blind, halted, or withered eyes that see how to walk in the fragrance that attracts His favor. May ignorance of the truth never stop, or hinder, you from the blessing that comes from walking in obedience.

Everyone is eligible for God's favor, sadly, not everyone qualifies. God does not play favorites; therefore, His favor is available to everyone. And, because favor is attached to a system, all people begin at the same level. He has given every person the same Bible along with the same opportunities to learn. However, the only ones who experience God's favor are those who learn to unlock His system.

The law of "Stewardship" is a system meant for all people. And, basically, John 5:4 is saying, "whosoever, got whatsoever they came for." Whosoever would get what was needed, at the time it was needed, if they were the first to enter the pool as the waters were stirred. This was a miracle producing system involving three steps. The first step was to be in the right place – be where it would be easy to get in the pool first. The second involved paying attention to the exact moment the waters began to stir. And the third step mandated being the first in the pool. If all three steps were followed, the miracle came forth. It did not matter who the person was, what race they were, or what they had done. If they worked the system, they got the reward. However, the Bethesda man did not fulfill the system, and yet, Jesus sought him out. Why? Because he did not pick a porch and he never quit on his miracle. For thirty-eight years, he continued his trek to the Bethesda pool. He did not camp on a porch with those who had given up; instead, he continued climbing towards his victory.

Favor is Seasonal

Blessings are seasonal and come through *windows of opportunity.* Pain is also seasonal while life is a continuous flow of seasons. Solomon, the wisest man who ever lived, stated, *"to everything there is a season."* Due to the formula for harvest being, "Seed-Time-Harvest (Genesis 8:22)," it is a mistake to believe, after sowing a seed, the reaping takes place immediately. Time and Season always stand between the seed and the harvest.

"For an angel went down __at a certain season...__" **(John 5:4 KJV)**

Because favor happens through process, it is important to understand, time is not the enemy. However, waiting can determine the proportion of favor granted. So, when the season of waiting is long, do not allow hopelessness or despair to hinder the scheduled, season of reaping. And, in order to walk in divine favor, it will be necessary to overcome the waiting season. It is possible to have a winning season, but favor is seasonal. And, in most cases, going through losing seasons will precede a winning one. Though, in the kingdom of God, it is, *"Sometimes you win, sometimes you LEARN, but you will never lose.*" This being the case, when in a delayed season and the blessing has not manifested, stay postured to receive. It is still on the way, so during the wait, do not allow the storms to shipwreck your faith, or your expectations. Instead, focus on the promises of God until this season passes. Isaiah 26:3 (NKJV) states, *"You will keep him in perfect peace, whose mind is stayed on You, because he trusts in You."* Feelings can cause people to let go of their expectations, so do not lose focus; *"Success isn't magic, or hocus pocus, success is simply learning how to focus."*

When Jesus saw him lie, and knew that he had been now a long time in that case, he saith unto him, wilt thou be made whole? 7 The impotent man answered him, Sir, I have no man, when the water is troubled, to put me into the pool: but while I am coming, another steps down before me. (John 5:6-7 KJV)

The Bethesda man was not born in his condition; however, during his life, something happened that caused this thirty-eight-year situation. It could have been anything, a sexually transmitted disease, witchcraft, who knows, however, sin never shares the consequences prior to the action. I once heard, *"Sin takes you farther than you wanted to go, keeps you longer than you planned on staying, and costs you far more than you were willing to pay."*

Afterward Jesus found him in the temple, and said to him, "See, you have been made well. Sin no more, lest a worse thing come upon you." (John 5:14 NKJV)

It is important to recognize, the Bethesda man's sin put him in this condition, not God. Jesus warned him to stop sinning so nothing worse would happen to him. It would not be God punishing him; however, the consequences of sin would be his punishment. After thirty-eight-years of suffering, it is vital he does not take his healing lightly. In other words, he must always remember to walk away from the sin that drove him to that pool.

You Are the Key to Favor

God decides favor; it is not connected to the actions of others but to the individual person's own actions. And, unfortunately, most people will not help another person get where they desire to be. Therefore, it will be necessary, in some cases, to forget being polite so he can push through the crowd. The Bethesda man told Jesus, *"Sir, I have no man, when the water is troubled, to put me into the pool: but while I am coming, another steps down before me.* (John 5:7 KJV) In the course of thirty-eight-years, how many times had he been pushed out of the way of his miracle? Did he stop being polite and start fighting for his position at the pool? I believe he realized no one would help him, so he began taking the initiative to win the battle for his healing; so, he stood on the side of the pool determined to get in first.

After being pushed around such a lengthy period, he not only needs a physical healing but an emotional one as well. Being hurt by a family member, a friend, a spouse, or a leader can create deep wounds of rejection which cause anger and distrust; they also cause feelings of emptiness and pain. I am sure this is exactly what the Bethesda man experienced as people stepped over, on, and around him to get in the pool first. Therefore, it is important to deal with these emotional wounds before becoming bitter and bound to anger. If not, a wall will form around the wound with the purpose of shutting people out. Initially, it is easy to act as though people are not being a bother, but as time goes on, the enemy will continue pouring salt on the wound. Then, as Satan gains a stronghold, isolation begins; it is a cave of loneliness, despair, depression, and defeat. These are things that typically drive people to God and church, however, they can have the opposite effect with people moving away from them. It is as the saying goes, *"Where you need to be the most, you are there the least. And, where you need to be the least, you are there the most."*

At times, life is hard and has a way of defeating a person's faith and expectations. Sadly, life must be endured as much as lived; however, persistence is the key to winning. People must make up their minds to always believe, pursue the end-goal, and never give up on themselves, or on God. This attitude creates a fragrance that attracts His attention as well as His favor.

Unfortunately, due to sin, the process of life involves pain and being hurt which cannot be helped. So, because of this, life is not always grandiose. Therefore, it is imperative people hold on to their faith in order to get through the troubled times. Remember the persistence of the Bethesda man. He kept going to the pool and he stayed in pursuit of his healing. He did not join himself to unbelievers who had given up but, instead, decided to live on the fifth porch – the porch of favor.

Last Thought

Please do not quit church; do not quit giving; and, do not quit praising, or worshiping, God. Most people quit when they are within a short timeframe of, their fragrance, attracting His favor. It could be as close as tomorrow, so hang on and continue believing that God is on His way. Remember, the waiting period can determine how large the harvest will be; and, because a miracle takes time, it will not manifest overnight. Continue the battle, *"for in due season we shall reap if we do not lose heart."*

(Galatians 6:9 NKJV) Thus, work your faith because faith works. Keep the Faith!

Finding the Field of Favor

Chapter 5

Laws That Alter Favor

Legislation is not only a group of people within the government of a nation, but it means the power to make LAW. Every country has its own legislation and laws; however, the law that works in one nation, will not work in another. Within the United States of America, every individual state has its own legislation. Therefore, not every law is the same for every state. For example, in North Carolina, it is legal to use a dashboard, radar detector but it is illegal in Virginia. I found this out the hard way. While driving into Virginia, I neglected to see the sign stating, "Radar Detectors, not legal in the State of Virginia." However, shortly after crossing the State line, into Virginia, a State Trooper with his blue lights on, pulled in behind me. Knowing I was not speeding, I was unsure of why he was pulling me over. It did not take long for the officer to inform me that I was in violation of Virginia's state law regarding radar detectors. Though I was not from Virginia, nor was my radar detector plugged in, I received a ticket for this infraction of their law. Therefore, I had to pay the fine. It is important to remember, "laws are set in place to protect people, not to punish them."

Favor is a Reaction for Something Done

Over time, I have learned while praying, not to pray for things like favor, success, or money. Although, it would make life much easier if this type of prayer worked. However, these things come as the result of decisions, actions, and reactions.

- *Favor is activated by action.* So, without action, favor is welfare! God's Word states, *"If a man will not work, he shall not eat."* This does not imply a welfare God.
- *Favor is activated by training*
- *Favor is activated through conversation*
- *Favor is activated through discoveries*

- *Favor is hidden in the life of a mentor*

With one moment of favor from the Pharoah of Egypt, Joseph's life was completely changed. After interpreting Pharoah's dream, Joseph was put in charge of Pharoah's house as well as over all the land of Egypt. Ruth also had a moment of favor when she allowed Naomi to be her mentor. It is interesting to note, God did not instruct Ruth to follow Naomi, nor did He tell her how to find Boaz. However, Ruth saw something in Naomi that caused her to believe she could follow her. Therefore, she left Moab, along with all its resources, to travel to Judah with Naomi. Through her counsel, Ruth learned to work the process of resource, discovery, provision, and promotion.

In another moment of favor, the widow of 2 Kings chapter four, learned of the treasures hidden within her own limited resources. Verse, one states, *"A certain woman of the wives of the sons of the prophets cried out to Elisha, saying, 'Your servant my husband is dead, and you know that your servant feared the Lord. And the creditor is coming to take my two sons to be his slaves.'"* In other words, her husband left her, heavily, in debt and the creditors were going to take her sons to pay off what she now owed. The prophet responds by asking, *"What shall I do for you? Tell me, what do you have in the house?"* Though, I am sure, she was shocked by the questions, he was working the process of overflow. He was seeking to determine if she had something of value in her house that she had overlooked. Again, probably with apprehension, she answered, *"Your maidservant has nothing in the house but a jar of oil."* (Verse 2 NKJV) That was the discovery needed for her life to change forever; it was the key that unlocked her provision.

Most people do not realize they possess something that can unlock their source of provision. It is impossible to count the times I missed out on the needed provision because I was not looking in the right place. On the other hand, after discovering some hidden treasures, I was able to turn them into a seed for what was needed. So, remember, one moment of favor can propel people into an accelerated future. Let me make this clear it is not necessary to have favor with everyone, but it is necessary to have favor with the right "somebody." Ruth did not need everyone in the field to favor her, she only needed Boaz.

The Laws of Favor

The Law of Integrity is doing what is right because it is the right thing to do. It is adherence to moral and ethical principles; soundness of moral character; and honesty. (Dictionary.com) This can be very difficult; because, due to fear of consequences, people will compromise the truth. However, when a person has a good reputation of telling the truth, and doing what was agreed upon, then, their integrity will attract favor. It is always important to follow through and to keep any agreements or promises because they matter.

Integrity is staying committed to the agreement even when the circumstances change. Unfortunately, the current standard, of this world, devalues truth while placing more value on winning than being honorable. Their mantra is, *"Win at all costs."* Nevertheless, favor is attracted to integrity before being attracted to a mere winner. Integrity will outlast dreams and will attract God's attention. So, do what you say; show up when you said; and, put action to your words. This will encourage favor in the place God has planted you.

The Law of Protocol is an established system of conduct, or etiquette; it gives honor to entry. That means there is a right way for people to enter the atmosphere of another, or certain conduct that protocol demands. It is important to honor the people allowed into your atmosphere. This can be done through expressions of gratitude and genuine smiles; standing up, handshakes, and hugs can also be proper. When done in sincerity, these gestures can create an atmosphere of honor which is appropriate in any environment. Unfortunately, this is easy to overlook when the relationship has been a long-standing one. In this case, it becomes necessary to prevent taking that relationship for granted; it might not be there forever. So, it is important to pay attention to protocol by, always, making the person feel welcome. And it is just as important for the person entering the room to honor the one giving access. This happens by entering their atmosphere, or office, with their permission; never barge in, especially if they are in another person's office.

Believe it, or not, there was a time protocol was taught to children. I remember, when I was young, my parents being very concerned about how my siblings, and I were to conduct ourselves. So, they taught us manners, posture, and how to address our elders along with respecting our teachers, leaders, as well as those in authority. This was done for us to be accepted, and respected, in the presence of all these people. We were taught to say, "Yes sir and yes ma'am," "May I be excused," "May I please have...," and "No thank-you." Sadly, this generation is lacking in protocol; they do not understand the respect necessary for entry, posture, or manners.

Protocol is so powerful that, without it, Satan cannot enter God's presence. It is therefore, feasible, that people can ignore protocol and miss the favor of God. And, *since He is a God of divine protocol*, it is impossible for people to stumble upon Him, or discover Him through worldly research.

God's protocol is simple
1. To have access to the Father, it is necessary to go through Jesus Christ; there is only one way to the Father. So, do not believe the lie that says there are many ways. And

disregard the hyper-grace doctrines which justify bad lifestyles as well as eliminates the need for personal responsibility, or repentance.

Jesus said to him, "I am the way, the truth, and the life. No one comes to the Father except through Me. (John 14:6 NKJV)

2. Enter God's presence, His gates, with *thanksgiving*. Otherwise, without a thankful heart, there is no getting through to His courts. Without this protocol, the angels of God will not allow entrance. Therefore, the key of entry is thankfulness.

Enter His gates with thanksgiving, and into His courts with praise. (Psalm 100:4 NKJV)

3. Enter His courts with *praise*. It is the act of expressing approval or admiration; the offering of grateful homage in words or song; or an act of worship. (Dictionary.com) Never underestimate this type of bold adoration because it opens the door into His presence.

Therefore, brethren, having boldness to enter the Holiest by the blood of Jesus... (Hebrews 10:19 NKJV)

... in whom we have boldness and confident access through faith in Him. (Ephesians 3:12)

4. Then, after thanksgiving and praise, offer all requests to God.

5. Seek God with a genuine heart and a mind of humility; an arrogant mindset keeps the door shut
6. Acknowledge all sin and repent.
7. Believe His Word, or Christ, who is truth; for, He is eternal life.
8. Surrender all, confess Jesus as Lord, and receive His forgiveness. And, according to 2 Corinthians 5:21, you are "now" the righteousness of God in Christ Jesus.

"For He made Him who knew no sin to be sin for us, that we might become the righteousness of God in Him." (NKJV)

(Matthew 6:33; John 1:1-14; John 14:6; Romans 10:9-13; 2 Corinthians 5:17-21; and 1 John 1:9)

Because God is a God of principles, nothing outside of that will ever work. It is impossible to enter His presence, or to attain His divine righteousness, with religious ideology, chanting, carnal meditation, individual beliefs of right and wrong, or secular works of charity. The only way to have an audience with the Father is through the door, Jesus Christ. It does not matter what people believe about this, or disbelieve, this IS God's protocol.

I am the door. If anyone enters by Me, he will be saved, and will go in and out and find pasture. **(John 10:9)**

Truth can never become a lie nor can a lie ever become truth; it does not matter how popular, or unpopular, either one may be, they will never change into something they are not. And, as God's creation, we are subject to His protocol and will be held accountable for how we followed, or rejected, it.

Two examples, in the Bible, of protocol include: 1) Esther entered a twelve-month preparation period prior to seeing King Ahasuerus. This included six-months with oil of myrrh and six-months with perfumes and preparations for beautifying women.

2) Daniel was trained for three-years to be interviewed by Nebuchadnezzar. In that three-years, he learned a new language, the literature of the Babylonians, their manners, and how to posture before the King of Babylon. They both followed protocol and God's hand of favor was upon them. And they did it while keeping their attitudes in check. If it was necessary for them to be trained in protocol, it is just as important for the people of this age to be trained as well. It would be very advantageous to learn, and practice, the protocol of entry unto our King.

The Law of Servanthood is the seed for recognition. Unfortunately, this word gives a negative mental picture of a servant, or a slave. However, this is about serving the interests of King Jesus. It is about identifying, or anticipating, a problem then resolving it. God favors a servant's heart; but, to say you are a servant, and being a servant, are two different things. One serves God from his heart while the other works for money; the latter is no longer a servant but an employee.

Servants

1. Immediately react when a need presents itself
2. Maintain the right tone of voice when asked to do something
3. Focus on serving rather than on themselves
4. Practice extending honor to others
5. Succeed where placed
6. Discomfort does not stop them from serving

7. Servanthood is a conversation, to God, about one's future
8. Serving explains a person's character and reveals their identity

Questions That Should be Asked

- What needs to be done?
- Am I in position to accomplish, or solve the problem?
- Will I do it with excellence?

The Law of Words is a powerful law because, most people, have no idea how powerful their words are. Throughout my life, there have been situations where I spoke words which got me into some very uncomfortable predicaments. And, because of the spiritual and mental wounds caused by those words, their pain could last a lifetime. For this reason, some would say, verbal abuse can be more damaging than physical abuse. The Bible says that a person who restrains his lips is wise, therefore, practicing the opposite makes one a fool. I would apply this same principle to what is posted on social media. Remember, cyber bullying, through the printed word, is just as damaging as hearing those same words spoken.

***In the multitude of words sin is not lacking, but he who restrains his lips is wise.* (Proverbs 10:19 NKJV)**

Words build bridges for people to cross, or they give the enemy access; they can represent, doors, walls, or bridges. Conversations can open doors to many opportunities including relationships, better jobs, even greater seasons. However, it is important to monitor what is said during those conversations because people are always listening; here is a word of wisdom,

"Silence can't be misquoted." While wrong words can bring about destruction, right words can turn any situation into a solution. The bible describes words as seed which, when spoken, are planted in a receptive mind. The conception between the mind, and the spoken word, will either produce success, or failure, in any situation in life. Therefore, it is necessary to guard your mind to prevent the planting of illegitimate ideas.

A word can create favor or stop favor in its tracks. Also, words reveal training so, when around other people, be aware of the words being spoken; they can change people for the better or they can beat them down. An unstoppable energy is created when releasing words of affirmation and appreciation, but the opposite happens when speaking words that cut.

Pleasant words are like a honeycomb, sweetness to the soul and health to the bones. (Proverbs 16:24 NKJV)

Death and life are in the power of the tongue, and those who love it will eat its fruit. (Proverbs 18:21 NKJV)

To the spirit, soul, mind, and body, the tongue is either a doorway to life, or it is a world of iniquity. It is the muscle that controls what goes into the body for nourishment; but it also controls the words that will feed the mind of others. With the tongue, it is possible, according to James 3:9, *"To bless our God and Father, or to curse men. Out of the same mouth proceed blessing and cursing which ought not to be."* The tongue can release blessings of affirmation, or compliments, or release curses that proceed from complaining. Depending on what is said, a team is either motivated to win or they are beat down and lose. Right words create momentum while harmful words suck the life out of the room; and wrong words can stop the progress of any great work.

It is important for people to pay, close attention to what is being spoken about oneself, and others; and, how often it is being said. Psalm 139:4 states, *"Even before there is a word on my tongue, behold, Lord, you know it all."* And those who speak words that represent death, or life, will either suffer, or enjoy, its consequences; no word escapes God's attention. So, do not trivialize any conversation, because *"when God wanted to change any season, He spoke."*

The Law of Reaction reveals who a person is during a crisis. In every aspect of life, either inward or outward, there are reactions that need to be, rightly, dealt with to live a life of favor. Otherwise, some reactions will influence, or shape, the next ten, twenty, or even fifty-years of the person's life whether good or bad. Some reactions are made unconsciously and seem to be as meaningless blips on the radar of life. From the first thought of the day, people are reacting to their environment. And, those reactions can happen without thought, or without purpose. Most reactions to stimuli are likely to happen in an unplanned event, such as, catching a falling fork. Or, they can be inconsequential, or insignificant, like changing the channel on the television. However, others are very significant in the role of one's future and must be taken seriously.

Every day, people are presented with new situations, events, challenges, and conversations meant to elicit reactions. For some, this will produce an emotional, volatile, irrational, spontaneous, or even disastrous attitude. While, for others, the reaction will be measured, calm, considerate, and strategic. Emotions are the vehicle that drive people, but the steering wheel should be logic and intelligence.

So, *why do people react stupidly when they should know better?* Unfortunately, "in the heat of the moment," most reactions are invariably lacking logic, understanding, or intelligence. Instead, their reactions are motivated by their emotions which are based in insecurity, anger, fear, resentment, or jealousy – just to name a few; all these come under the banner of "feelings." And, feelings prevent people from logically thinking through situations before reacting. Now, instead of controlling their reactions, their feelings are controlling them. Therefore, previous prayers, studies, and self-help guides go out the window – *"Been there, done that, and I bought the t-shirt."* It is easy to be in control when situations are not demanding a reaction, however, when a crisis sneaks in, so does the test. And, the test reveals whether, or not, the person's reactions have been mastered.

People who control their reactions, even during betrayal, or when frustrated and overwhelmed, are those who have mastered their feelings and emotions. *Favor is attracted to right reaction,* which enables people to succeed when others cannot. It is important to note, mastering reaction involves allowing the mind to be in control rather than feelings or emotions. And, when feelings are mastered, reactions will be as well. Again, *"I can't always control what is happening around me, however, I can always control what is happening in my mind."*

- React for the results desired
- Reaction determines longevity of an offense
- Reaction decides the size of the problem
- Reaction decides who is allowed in
- Reaction unlocks the law of precession - (preceding) an emotion

How an individual reacts to correction, rejection, loss, or an adversary determines their focus. Reaction magnifies; therefore, in all situations, it is necessary to practice the proper way to react to be attracted to favor.

The Law of opportunity is an appropriate, or favorable time, for a set of circumstances to help make success possible. Because favor is attached to opportunity, it is important to recognize every timely, moment. It is said, *"One person's problem is another person's opportunity."* My mentor knew of a businessman who was dealing with a particular situation, and, because he was equipped to help him, this issue was resolved. As a result, the businessman sent him a check for $135,000.00; his problem became an opportunity for my mentor.

Pain is an Opportunity for Learning

Pain is an indicator of something out of order so, do not hate or fear it, use it. It is a built-in alarm system meant for the individual to stop and take inventory. This is an opportunity to seek discovery to make changes. Pain, or a problem, can be a door to hidden success. So, learn to look for opportunities in every situation, such as:

- Famine is an opportunity for change
- Correction is an opportunity for growth
- Anger is an opportunity for self-control

The Law of Gratitude is an attitude of the heart. Saying "thank you" does not mean the person is grateful nor does it mean he has a grateful heart. I struggle with this and, at times, am ungrateful. One reason people tend to be ungrateful is they believe they deserve more. And, it is easy to carry a thankless attitude when discouraged. Sadly, anger and failure follow those who are ungrateful. However, success has its foundation in gratitude.

Having a thankful attitude brings multiplication into one's life. It is the seed for more and it replenishes the atmosphere for additional miracles to take place. God loves to favor those who are thankful. Thus, in the Bible, when the woman with the issue of blood was healed, in reverence, she told Jesus the whole truth of what had happened to her. I believe she was grateful, or deeply appreciative, of the healing she received. After this healing, Jesus was informed that the synagogue ruler's daughter had died; He was setup for another miracle. Gratitude carries a force, of power, that prevents anything on earth, or below, from stopping its ability to multiply. So, it is to every individual's benefit to exercise as well as maintain a grateful attitude.

The Law of Adaptation reveals strength. It is the seed that grows the harvest of favor in every environment; it is the ability to adapt oneself to different conditions. It was once said that dinosaurs went extinct because they could not adapt. However, cockroaches and alligators learned to adapt and have been on earth for thousands of years. Therefore, staying adaptable will place individuals in the audience of great people. As an example, the people, of Egypt, recognized that Joseph had a different spirit. He learned the power of adaptation and practiced it while in the middle of his circumstances, thus, was brought before Pharoah.

The way to win in this world, I believe, is by being adaptable; this is the influence necessary for people to reach their own greatness. People will never win by building walls through arguing. However, conversation builds bridges. Bridges are important for maneuvering through the enemy's camp to establish kingdom success. God will favor those who are able to adapt without being consumed by the views, values, and opinions of those in opposition.

Remember, the whole world, along with its systems, operates through laws. So, study and practice these eight laws and watch His favor show up.

Finding the Field of Favor

Chapter 6

Favor Produces Prosperity

Where there is honor, there is favor...and, where there is favor, there is prosperity... there is money!

It is hard to understand, knowing it is God's desire, why people get angry and hostile over His followers becoming prosperous. Why would they shut out a message which shows God's intent for people to have, yes, money? The Bible plainly says in 3 John 2, *"Beloved, I pray that you may prosper in all things..."* Money is included in "all things." So, if money were the enemy, it would not be necessary to have a job. However, it is needed in order to pay bills, buy food, clothes, a home, a car, along with many other things. Therefore, money is a vehicle for increase and convenience.

Money is a tool to help people stay in their preferred lifestyle. Therefore, it does not make sense that people get upset when finding out they can have more. And, just because a few have abused the principle, does not make the message wrong. The truth is the truth; it cannot be altered, or compromised, even for selfish gain. Otherwise, if it could, then stop teaching the prosperity message and see what happens. Chaos will not be far behind. This kind of a mindset will cause people to misplace the true value, or power, contained within the truth of prosperity. As a result, the benefits of a prosperous life and financial freedom are lost.

Again, prosperity is a tool used to help people succeed in life; it is not the enemy. However, my question becomes, "how can people help others if they are always in need, or they are covered up with debt?" Being prosperous will not only meet personal needs but it can also eliminate debt. The resulting surplus can be distributed to others to help them get to their place of prosperity as well; this is called, "Being a Blessing."

To me, the salvation message IS the prosperity message. John 10:10 states, *"...I have come that they may have life, and that they may have it more abundantly."* This does not say anything about survival or barely getting by. He said He came to give us an abundant life, not an average one. And, to have abundance means to have an extremely plentiful or oversufficient quantity or supply. Does that suggest poverty? Throughout the Bible, Jesus taught about the Kingdom of God This is a message of:

- Salvation
- Deliverance
- Change
- Prosperity

Favor is God's endorsement; and, whatever He endorses, the devil cannot deny. Therefore, whoever He favors will prosper. *"God's favor always produces prosperity."* And, prosperity is much bigger than money. However, money is included in the bigger picture of what God intends for prosperity. This word has multiple meanings in the Bible:

- Well-being
- Happiness
- Good health
- Wholeness
- Financial freedom

Therefore, the spirit of hell is the one thing that will attack the message of financial freedom; this message is capable of freeing people to fulfill their destiny. The devil does not want the prosperity message spoken from the pulpit of the church. He would prefer a salvation message of survival only. However, God desires that people thrive under His Kingdom theology. Because Holy Spirit inspired the word, in 3 John 2, He really does desire people to prosper in "all things." Therefore, He desires that His people be blessed in order to be a blessing to others. Prosperity is the truth while poverty, or debt, is the lie.

God's Word is Clear on Prosperity

Sing unto the LORD, O ye saints of his, and give thanks at the remembrance of his holiness. 5) For his anger endured but a moment; in his favor is life: weeping may endure for a night, but joy cometh in the morning. 6) **And in my prosperity, I said, I shall never be moved.** *7) LORD, by thy favor thou hast made my mountain to stand strong: thou didst hide thy face, and I was troubled.* **(Ps 30:4-7 KJV)**

  Because favor is life, or prosperity, people can say, *"I shall never be moved."* In all situations, due to His hand of favor, they have stability. And, favor makes people strong. It also prevents them from becoming weak, or feeble.

27) Let them shout for joy, and be glad, that favour my righteous cause: yea, let them say continually, Let the LORD be magnified, which hath **pleasure in the prosperity of his servant.** *28) And my tongue shall speak of thy righteousness and of thy praise all the daylong.* **(Ps 35:27-28 KJV)**

  Favor also produces incredible joy; it induces moments of singing and shouting praises unto God. Or, magnifying the Lord. Therefore, when God favors His people, prosperity is released as well. Psalm 35:27 says, *"SHOUT FOR JOY!"* Why? Because He takes pleasure in our prosperity. The Lord loves seeing His children walk under the umbrella of His blessing. And, He is thrilled when they receive His hand of favor.

25) Save now, I beseech thee, O LORD: O LORD, I beseech thee, send now prosperity. 26) Blessed be he that cometh in the name of the LORD: we have blessed you out of the house of the LORD. **(Psalm 118:25 KJV)**

In this verse, God's people pray that He send prosperity. When? Now! Notice, this blessing comes from the "house of the Lord." However, because His house is not always the focus, many people miss out on His prosperity. They say, "I love the Lord," but their weekly attendance is very weak (pun intended). It is sad, but almost anything can take precedence over His house. It is very sad. Again, the word says, *"We have blessed you out of the house of the Lord."* The house is where God's people gather to bless Him. Therefore, when He is blessed, He covers them with His favor.

6) Pray for the peace of Jerusalem: they shall prosper that love thee. 7) Peace be within thy walls, and prosperity within thy palaces. 8) For my brethren and companions' sakes, I will now say, Peace be within thee. 9) Because of the house of the LORD our God I will seek thy good. (Psalm 122:6-9 KJV)

In the day of prosperity be joyful. (Ecclesiastes 7:14 KJV)

I spake unto thee in thy prosperity; but thou saidst, I will not hear. This hath been thy manner from thy youth, that thou obeyedst not my voice. (Jeremiah 22:21 KJV)

Cry yet, saying, thus saith the LORD of hosts; My cities through prosperity shall yet be spread abroad; and the LORD shall yet comfort Zion, and shall yet choose Jerusalem. (Zechariah 1:17 KJV)

If they obey and serve him, they shall spend their days in prosperity, and their years in pleasures. 12) But if they obey not, they shall perish by the sword, and they shall die without knowledge. (Job 36:11-12 KJV)

These are a few scriptures regarding prosperity; they are awesome in that they carry His power and influence. Because they can liberate from lack and poverty, the enemy would rather they be ignored. However, through reading, re-reading, memorizing, remembering, and confessing them, they can overturn the enemy's agenda and bring in God's prosperity.

The question then becomes, "how much favor can one expect from the Lord?" Whatever is needed to fulfill His purpose. People should live for God with the same exuberance as they once did for the enemy. In other words, whatever depths one sank to as a sinner, should be the heights risen to in His Kingdom. Therefore, if building a skyscraper is the goal, then digging deep into the soil and laying the proper foundation is necessary. And, this struggle will be the determining factor of one's greatness.

HOW TO INCREASE FAVOR

- Wisdom decides the level of favor
- Favor changes seasons
- Faith decides divine timing

***Let thy mercy, O LORD, be upon us, according as we hope in thee.* (Psalm 33:22 KJV)**

This formula has the power to increase a person's life; therefore, it is necessary to, first, seek wisdom through His Word. As I did this, I discovered Proverbs 8:35 which states, *"He who finds 'Me' finds 'Life' and receives 'Favor' from the Lord."* Who is the "Me" in this verse? The answer to this question is the key to all prosperity. Verse one of this same chapter states, *"Does not wisdom cry out?"* Then, the rest of the chapter reveals wisdom's purpose. Therefore, the "Me," in this verse, is wisdom. Wisdom is the Spirit of Jesus. It is Holy Spirit, the One who knows all things and who guides people through every situation in life. However, it is not knowledge, nor is it information.

But of Him you are in Christ Jesus, who became for us wisdom from God. **(1 Corinthians 1:30 KJV)**

When anyone discovers Holy Spirit is the voice of all wisdom, it helps them obtain favor from the Lord. And, whatever He touches, God endorses. John 16:7 states, *"Nevertheless I tell you the truth. It is to your advantage that I go away; for if I do not go away, the Helper will not come to you; but if I depart, I will send Him to you."* The word *advantage* means benefit; gain; or profit. It is any state, circumstance, opportunity, or means especially favorable to success, interest, or any desired end. It is a position of superiority; and means to cause to advance or to promote. *(Dictionary.com)* Because, Holy Spirit is the spirit of wisdom, it is to people's advantage to walk with Him. Proverbs 8 tells us about wisdom, and verse thirty-five changed my whole life. Therefore, I encourage you to read the entire chapter.

Does not wisdom cry out, and understanding lift up her voice? 2) She takes her stand on the top of the high hill, beside the way, where the paths meet. 3) She cries out by the gates, at the entry of the city, at the entrance of the doors: 4) To you, O men, I call, and my voice is to the sons of men. 5) O you simple ones, understand prudence, and you fools, be of an understanding heart. 6) Listen, for I will speak of excellent things, and from the opening of my lips will come right things; 7) For my mouth will speak truth; wickedness is an abomination to my lips. 8) All the words of my mouth are with righteousness; nothing crooked or perverse is in them. 9) They are all plain to him who understands, and right to those who find knowledge. 10) Receive my instruction, and not silver, and knowledge rather than gold; 11) For wisdom is better than rubies, and all the things one may desire cannot be compared with her. 12) I, wisdom, dwell with prudence, and find out knowledge and discretion. 13) The fear of the Lord is to hate evil; pride and arrogance and the evil way and the perverse mouth I hate. 14) Counsel is mine, and sound wisdom; I am understanding, I have strength. 15) By me kings reign, and rulers decree justice. 16) By me princes' rule, and nobles, all the judges of the earth. 17) I love those who love me, and those who seek me diligently will find me. 18) Riches and honor are with me, enduring riches and righteousness. 19) My fruit is better than gold, yes, than fine gold, and my revenue than choice silver. 20) I traverse the way of righteousness, in the midst of the paths of justice, 21) That I may cause those who love me to inherit wealth, that I may fill their treasuries. 22) The Lord possessed me at the beginning of His way, before His works of old. 23) I have been established from everlasting, from the beginning, before there was ever an earth. 24) When there were no depths, I was brought forth, when there were no fountains abounding with water. 25) Before the mountains were settled, before the hills, I was brought forth; 26) While as yet He had not made the earth or the fields, or the primal dust of the world. 27) When He prepared the heavens, I was there, when He drew a circle on the face of the deep, 28) When He established the clouds above, when He strengthened the fountains of the deep, 29) When He assigned to the sea its limit, so that the waters would not transgress His command, when He marked out the foundations of the earth, 30) Then I was beside Him as a master craftsman; and I was daily His delight, rejoicing always before Him, 31) Rejoicing in His inhabited world, and my delight was with the sons of men. 32) Now therefore, listen to me, my children, for blessed are those who keep my ways. 33) Hear instruction and be wise, and do not disdain it. 34) Blessed is the man who listens to me, watching daily at my gates, waiting at the posts of my doors. 35) For whoever finds me finds life, and obtains favor from the Lord: 36) But he who sins against me wrongs his own soul; all those who hate me love death. **(Proverbs 8 NKJV)**

This says, when a person increases in wisdom, God will also increase the favor in his life.

- Wisdom determines the level of favor,
- Favor schedules seasons,
- And, faith decides divine timing.

After presenting this formula, during a church service, a wheelchair bound man, with an oxygen tank, jumped up and ran around the room; he was completely healed.

Wisdom decides the level of favor I walk in. *Favor changes seasons...faith decides divine timing.* And, the bible is clear, *"Without faith it is impossible to please God."* Why? Because faith is confidence in God. It is not possible to, successfully, make it through a crisis without having a strong confidence in Him.

One purpose of favor is to change seasons; and, with God's favor, the season begins changing immediately. Though it might not look, or feel, like changes are occurring, be assured, they are. They, typically, start in the unseen realm, then work their way into the seeing realm where people can observe them. Just as the song states, *"Even when you cannot see it, He is working, even when you cannot feel it, He is working... He never stops, never stops working."* For this reason, it is important to

95

keep believing. So, do not let go of faith. No matter how devasting the situation appears, God does not see it that way. Keep Believing! Otherwise, if allowed, the enemy will use the storms of life to shipwreck the faith necessary for success. Therefore, with bulldog tenacity, build yourself up in your most holy faith and keep believing.

Life in God's Mercy

Mercy is God's love, or forgiveness, manifested. It is not pity from God but how He favors His people. Psalm 33:22 states, *"Let Your mercy, O Lord, be upon us, just as we hope in You."* Hope is more than wishing, it is a mental stability that decides favor. Hell cannot kill this kind of expectation in the promises of God. Hope, constantly, anticipates His outcome in any trial. It is a bridge that moves people, from a bad place, to a better place.

- From despair to devotion,
- Problems to promotion,
- Anger to adoration,
- Pain to praise,
- Past to future, and
- Failure to faithfulness.

Hope keeps favor alive; it is the substance of faith. Again, wisdom determines one's level of favor while favor changes a season. But it is faith that decides divine timing. And, for faith to have substance, in the present, hope must be maintained. Chapter eleven, of Hebrews, says that faith is the substance of things hoped for, or expected. Faith is the expectation of being healed. So, the greater the level of expectation one walks in will determine the favor received.

Therefore, hope is expectation placed on faith. And, great faith produces great favor. Thus, people do not always have everything they need because God wants everyone to trust Him for increase. And, because God is the Source of every good and perfect thing, He wants to be recognized as such.

Prosperity is the fruit of favor, unfortunately, the religious always attempt to succeed without God. They wait to call on God when they are trapped, or when they do not know how to get free. Sadly, religious people are everywhere. They are recognized by their selfishness – selfish gain and self-promotion included. The religious use God's promises like witches' incantations and they hide their intentions with religious words and actions. However, comfort and individual gain are their motivations. The Lord will never allow people to be "religious" *completely alone*. He has a way of making them realize that, without Him, true success is impossible to achieve. Therefore, seasons of loss are scheduled for the purpose of waking the individual to the reality of unrighteous motivations. Using God for one's own purposes is never the way of increase, however, serving Him is of great benefit.

God Never Rescues People Without Favoring Them

When God was preparing Moses to be the deliverer of His people, He said,
"And I am sure that the king of Egypt will not let you go, no, not by a mighty hand." **(Exodus 3:19 KJV)**

As God instructs Moses with what he is to ask Pharoah, He also tells Him what to expect. God informed Moses that Pharoah would not let His people go and there was nothing he could do to make it happen. Basically, God was saying, "No matter how hard you pray, how hard you fight, or how hard you try not to fight, you will not succeed by your own might." Not even a "mighty hand" would turn things around.

Abilities, Without God, Will Not Produce Favor

If a person's talents, abilities, or intelligence could decide favor, then it is not divine favor. However, partnership with "Someone" greater produces provision, resources, and access needed for success. In Moses case, God instructed him to confront Pharoah but then, told him that Pharoah would not be intimidated by his request. Though God told him Pharoah would say no to his request, he was instructed to ask anyway. At that point, God revealed His strategy to Moses: take what is in your hand and let me add my power to it. Moses' behavior is an example, for today, of the biggest key to living a life of favor.

20) And I will stretch out my hand and smite Egypt with all my wonders which I will do in the midst thereof: and after that he will let you go. 21) And I will give this people favor in the sight of the Egyptians: and it shall come to pass, that, when ye go, ye shall not go empty. **(Exodus 3:20-21 KJV)**

God also instructed Moses in how the whole ordeal would end, *"I will give this people favor."* In other words, He was telling Moses that the ending would be better than the beginning. So, do not fear but stay encouraged. And, rather than reacting to fear, make the decision to be courageous during the showdown. God endorsed Moses; therefore, he would be granted favor. Remember, whatever God favors, hell cannot stop. Thus, whatever is impossible through man's wisdom, might, or abilities, God's favor can accomplish supernaturally.

Therefore, hold on to God's promises, the struggle is not in vain. Because favor and promotion are on the way, being empty-handed is not an option. So, when the people come out of their bondages, they will walk away with the wealth of their enemies. And, the same God, who delivered the people of Israel from the Pharoah of Egypt, is still delivering people today. Also, as Israel left Egypt, covered with a cloud by day and a pillar of fire by night, they never had to plunder while in the wilderness. God provided everything necessary for their journey to the promised land. It is amazing how God's favor will supply everything needed when His vision is prioritized. I say, *"Provision for the vision."*

Favor is not money; it is much bigger than that. However, money is present when favor is released. *"Favor always produces financial harvest."* Sadly, in the church arena, money is one of the most misunderstood of commodities. Fundamentalists go so far as to say that having money is evil and it is wrong. They assume it was obtained through some form of fraud. Therefore, when prosperity is preached, people want money left out of that message.

These are my questions, "If money is so evil, why do people keep it when they get it?" "Why don't they, immediately, get rid of it?" "Why don't they use it to advance the Kingdom of God?" "Wouldn't it make sense to turn over something perceived as evil to God and His work?" These questions may sound silly, but the religious church sounds just as silly when they proclaim that God is not concerned about money. Thankfully, God is very concerned about the financial prosperity of the church. Money, in and of itself, is not evil. Money in the hands of the righteous will produce righteousness, but money in the hands of the wicked produces wickedness.

Within the church, one of the products of money is the harvest of souls, for the Kingdom of God. It takes money to do the work of the gospel. The gospel message contains the power to deliver and set people free from sin as well as their bondages of sickness, disease, and poverty of spirit and soul. It is through the gospel message that whole congregations are transformed at the area of their need. Therefore, when money is added to the equation, the gospel message is spread further than the four walls of a building. It can impact a greater number of people simply because it was given for a righteous cause. Without money, the gospel would be limited to what people could do in their local communities.

- *Money amplifies.* Example, when drug addicts obtain money, their addiction is amplified.
- *Money creates convenience.* Convenience is the state of being able to proceed with something with little effort or difficulty. It is anything that saves or simplifies work; it adds to one's ease or comfort. When the real purpose of money is understood, it makes life much easier.
- *Money decides freedom.* Unfortunately, Satan has mastered this power. The world gets richer while the church becomes poorer.
- *Money makes growth easier.* Money gives a business the power it needs to grow. How? It allows them to purchase advertising, build better offices, buy up-to-date equipment, and hire more qualified employees. No other resource, when properly used, can manifest such power.
- *Money creates increase.* In the right market, or atmosphere, money will grow and increase at an incredible rate. Money increases better than it spends; the world understands this more than the church. Many nightclubs, hotels, and amusement parks are owned by the wicked. And, television stations that promote gross evil are also owned by the wicked. They have figured out how to spend millions of dollars to influence people, as well as their children, to spend money on their services.

Yet, in the local church, it is nearly impossible to raise enough funds to send the youth to Christian camps. Because of the increased poverty of those who occupy the pews, it is impossible to build schools that can equip people to advance in the marketplace. As a result, the church is losing members while the world is gaining new converts. God has given people the power that makes wealth, so why doesn't the church have more money? This is a question that should be answered for the church to be able to handle the increase God wants them to have.

God Does Not Give According to a Person's Prayers, He Gives According to What He Can Manage

The inability to manage money is the number one reason people do not have it. God will not increase what cannot be managed; so, managing what is presently available is key to having more. To manage means to handle, direct, govern, or control in action or use. It means to be in charge. Therefore, if people are not currently managing the money they already have, it may be necessary to get assistance before going to next level of increase. Ask hard questions like, "If I had more money, could I govern it well?" "If not, what am I willing to do in order to take charge of what I currently have?" Increase managing skills and the money will come.

Sadly, most people, who claim to be Christians, do not tithe. Only ten percent bring their tithes to the local church. These statistics are staggering because tithing is a kingdom key to increase. *First*, we do not have the right to keep the tithe because it belongs to God. *Secondly*, tithing is giving honor, or recognition, to the One who is our Source. Today, if I had a dollar for every time someone asked me why their financial ends do not meet, I would be rich. Usually, the answer stems from not tithing. And, the most common excuse is, "I can't afford to tithe." Although people cannot afford not to tithe. Their refusal to bring tithes into the local church is costly to their financial position.

In the past, people have approached me requesting prayer for their lottery ticket to be the big winner. They proclaim, "If I win, I will bring half of my winnings to the church." However, they were already neglecting to bring their tithes, from their weekly paychecks, into the storehouse. I am pretty sure, if their ticket won, the church would have seen little, if any, of the winnings.

It is a fact, *"the more a person has, the harder it is to tithe."* People get attached to their money so, for some, giving one-hundred dollars is easier than for others. Then, as increase happens, giving five-hundred dollars, or a thousand dollars becomes much more emotional. This has been the case for many who have received promotions from their jobs. Instead of bringing the new tithe amount, they quit coming to church. Luke 16:10 states, *"He who is faithful in what is least is faithful also in much; and he who is unjust in what is least is unjust also in much."* This tells us, if a person is not tithing on what they currently have, they will not tithe when they gain more; the opposite is also true. Also, Malachi 3:10 states, *"Bring all the tithes into the storehouse, that there may be food in My house, and try Me now in this, see if I will not open for you the windows of heaven and pour out for you such blessing that there will not be room enough to receive it."* Therefore, when God can trust you with tithing, He will overwhelm you with more."

Chapter 7

Enemies
Of
Favor

Ignorance

Ignorance will stop the flow of favor; it is not what you know that is killing you, it is what you do not know. This does not mean people are stupid, or unable to learn, it is simply a lack of the right knowledge. Ignorance occurs when people decide not to listen, therefore, even though the times have changed, they do not. It keeps people stuck in tradition, or the past, rather than motivating them to seek a new vision for their future.

Ignorance is the proof that people do not want to learn while stagnation is the harvest. It is the stuck mindset that will not allow room for new teaching or training. And, as wisdom would say, "move quickly away from those who refuse to keep up." Because technology rapidly changes, it is important for companies to stay up to date on those changes to compete in the marketplace. Change is inevitable, it cannot be stopped. Since stagnation is the harvest of ignorance, progress is the harvest of well-planned outgrowth. Therefore, change is the price paid for progress while ignorance interferes with any potential for increase.

I have learned, there are two things required for growth, synergy and flow. Synergy is the ability to get in step with others while flow is the by-product of synergy. A dance team will practice long hours to develop synergy; they learn how to come together in such a way they are able to anticipate the other's movements. They develop fluidity or, what the bible calls, unity. In other words, *synergy is combined effort*. Combined effort! Therefore, to grow in a competitive industry, the combined work, and efforts, of the whole team is necessary. And, when synergy is effective between staff and leaders or workforce and employers, one vision begins to flow.

Synergy is defined as, "the interaction or cooperation of two or more organizations, substances, or other agents to produce a combined effect greater than the sum of their separate effects." It is the power of a group moving in the same direction, with the same focus, and with one vision in mind, while flow is the harvest of synergy. This is demonstrated when a couple is unified within their marriage. Or, water, combined with current, creates flow. *Flow is the power of movement going in the same direction.* When water and current come together, as one, it can transform into a dangerous force and power; *the History Channel and the Weather Channel* frequently broadcast the power of flooded riverbanks. These waters will beat on structures until they are so weakened, they collapse and are permanently destroyed. This is also the case with corporations and organizations; when they become one unit, or when unity defines them, they can accomplish greater things in the marketplace. Therefore, it is important to remember, *ignorance can stop the power of synergy and flow.*

How good and pleasant it is when brothers live together in unity! 2) It is like precious oil poured on the head, running down on the beard, running down on Aaron's beard, down upon the collar of his robes. 3) It is as if the dew of Hermon were falling on Mount Zion. For there the LORD bestows his blessing, even life forevermore. **(Ps 133:1-3 NIV)**

Disobedience

The proof of trust is obedience. On the other hand, disobedience cripples one's ability to walk in divine favor. Disobedience reveals a lack of trust regarding to God's instructions. Unfortunately, people tend to forget there is a price to pay for disobedience. While obedience brings reward, pain can be the

105

consequence of disobeying an instruction. When I was growing up, I paid the price for disobedience; my parents did not put up with rebellion or dishonor. And, I had teachers who would punish their students for being disobedient to the classroom rules and instructions. I was taught to obey without hesitation and my feelings were never a factor in whether, or not, I obeyed. However, the consequences always kept me in check. I understood the rewards that came with obedience and I, also, knew there would be punishment if I rebelled against what I was told.

God never consults a person's feelings when giving an instruction. When I was growing up, the prerequisite to freedom was obedience. I recognized, early on, because of being obedient throughout the week, my dad was gracious to me on the weekends; obedience truly made my life easier. His favor came to me in the form of money for dates or gas for my car. Obedient children are always the recipients of the father's favor. Then, after enduring a season of instruction and correction, a new season of favor will follow.

God will never take a person beyond their last act of disobedience.

It is a fact; God will not take a person from one place, into another, while living a life of disobedience. And, until the lesson of obedience is learned, the current season could be a permanent one. It is important to note, hesitation is a form of disobedience. So, when God speaks, ACT!

***If they obey and serve Him (God), they will end their days in prosperity, and their years in pleasure.* (Job 36:11 NKJV)**

If you are willing and obedient, you shall eat the good of the land; (Isaiah 1:19 NKJV)

Obedience is, therefore, a key to God's favor. When the Lord sees a person's acts of obedience, He knows He can trust them. This was the case when God decided to take Abraham to the next level. The test came with this request, *"Take now your son, your only son Isaac, whom you love, and go to the land of Moriah, and offer him there as a burnt offering on one of the mountains of which I shall tell you."* (Genesis 22:2 NKJV) God saw, through his willingness and through his obedience to the request, that Abraham could be trusted with more. Verse nine states, *"Then they came to the place of which God had told him. And Abraham built an altar there and placed the wood in order; and he bound Isaac his son and laid him on the altar, upon the wood. 10) And Abraham stretched out his hand and took the knife to slay his son."* God will always qualify those He endorses.

Keys to divine increase include:
- Submission
- Sensitivity
- Separation
- Supplying your own way
- Surrender
- Switch
- Substitute

Upon hearing those instructions, though Abraham did not agree with God, he decided to submit, or act, to fulfill that request anyway. *When agreement ends, submission begins.* It is easy to submit when there is agreement in the instructions, however, it becomes a decision when agreement is not there. I am sure Abraham was completely against sacrificing his only son, but he decided to trust God instead of his feelings. When this decision was made, then acted upon, God knew Abraham could be trusted. Therefore, it is important to know, people will not always understand God's instructions, nor will they agree with them. However, it is vital to obey His words even when they make no sense.

Submission is the power and proof of obedience. Obedience opens the windows of heaven while disobedience will shut those windows and stop the flow of God's favor.

Submission is not weakness! Unfortunately, submission can be viewed as weakness. However, most great leaders began by being submissive to another leader. They either helped others gain success or they became students of those who had already acquired great accomplishments.

To be a servant involves having a strong sense of security. When leader and servant are walking in agreement, both are responsible for the cost and outcome of their journey. However, when coming to the crossroad of disagreement, the servant must take on the role of submission. This decision will disqualify him from the consequences due to a wrong outcome and, instead, qualify him for the harvest. In other words, submission to a leader takes the risk off the servant and places it directly onto the one who gave the instructions.

Specifically, to walk in agreement, the servant must be willing to follow an instruction even if not in full agreement. By submitting, under these conditions, they are entitled to the spoils, if the leader made the right decision. However, if the risk turns bad, then the leader bears the brunt of his mistake. Thus, the servant qualifies for the spoils while disqualifying for the losses due to the leader making a wrong choice. This is awesome! When submitting to God, this is awesome. However, it is important to exercise wisdom when following the instructions of man.

If people could understand this principle, it would slow down the exodus in most organizations. Unfortunately, most people believe that agreement Is submission, which is not the case. As an example, when people disagree with church leadership, they will leave assuming they were always in submission. Yet, that is not true. They were struggling with coming into agreement, but not in submission. Remember, *submission can only begin when agreement ends.* Because they were not in agreement with the leadership, they chose to leave rather than submit until seeing the result.

Covetousness

To covet means to wrongfully desire what belongs to another person; it is an attitude of never being satisfied with one's own lot in life, or their possessions. A covetous person is always evaluating what others have and comparing it to theirs. This never ends well because that comparison is *always from one person's weaknesses to another person's strengths.* When this takes place, the one making the comparison will feel lesser and will be tempted to compete instead of focusing on the completion of their divine assignment. Wrongfully coveting what others have can destroy churches, marriages, businesses, and relationships. And it can also destroy friendships.

"You shall not covet your neighbor's house. You shall not covet your neighbor's wife, or his manservant or maidservant, his ox or donkey, or anything that belongs to your neighbor." **(Exodus 20:17 NIV)**

"You shall not covet your neighbor's wife. You shall not set your desire on your neighbor's house or land, his manservant or maidservant, his ox or donkey, or anything that belongs to your neighbor." (Deuteronomy 5:21 NIV)

To be delighted in the goods and wealth of others is covetousness. And, when a person covets what their neighbor has, they could be suffering from identity depravation. They tend to lack self-confidence as well as self-worth. Therefore, when they compare themselves to others, it is difficult for them to enjoy what they have...cars, homes, businesses, vacations, marriages, etc. This leads to a dissatisfaction with their place in life, a place devoid of any peaceful moment of self-power. Many people have experienced this. One day they feel good about their life. The next day, after seeing their neighbor drive by in a brand-new car, they feel like a failure. Then, suddenly, the desire for a new car overwhelms them causing unwanted frustration and lack of fulfillment, a side effect of covetousness. And, sadly, this can lead to bad decisions which can, ultimately, create debts they are unable to repay.

Covetousness will stop the flow of favor.

Greed

Greed is an excessive desire for wealth or possessions; and is another word that describes coveting. These two words are like brothers. Though greed is the opposite of coveting, they walk hand in hand. The proof of greed is the inability of letting something go. It is allowing the property to be the owner rather than the other way around. Other words that describe greed include excess, gluttony, longing, selfishness, and indulgence.

Satan steals… Man hordes… God gives!

Greed is revealed every day in our churches. By applying this concept to money, we can see that money owns people rather than people giving money instructions in what to do. Therefore, people do not bring their tithes into the storehouse; they are not willing to let go of what belongs to God. This is Greed! And, when this spirit is working in a church, it manifests through the anger people feel when asked to let go of what they want to keep for themselves. There is an obvious transition from a joyful, uplifting, worship service to a mournful atmosphere at the mention of tithes and offerings. Maybe, it is a type of funeral service. Could it be the burying of the "god of greed" as the tithes are released into the house of God?

With the understanding that everything belongs to God and that He is the Source of all resource, it would seem, people would bring their tithes, with joy, back to the King of kings. Sadly, this is not always the case. However, the quickest cure for greed is giving. *Giving is a sure sign that you have conquered the spirit of greed.* Giving is also a sure sign that a person has the Lord's generous spirit. After all, *God is the biggest of all givers!* He gave the world His best offering, His Son, Jesus. And we are told to imitate God, therefore, we are to give Him our best as well.

Pride

God resists the proud, but He gives grace to the humble. Pride is a high opinion of one's own importance; their ego is so strong, no one can help them. And, prideful people are not teachable. Pride has three-sides: self-absorbed, character, and civic. It can be either positive or negative and produces excellence or judgment; God favors one while He curses the other.

The first side of pride is self-absorption. It is a high or inordinate opinion of one's own dignity, importance, merit, or superiority, whether as cherished in the mind or as displayed in bearing, conduct, etc. It is next to impossible to reach, or lead, an individual who thinks more highly of himself than he does of others.

***God opposes the proud but gives grace to the humble.* (James 4:6 NKJV)**

***I say to the boastful, 'Do not boast, and to the wicked, do not lift up your horn'* (Psalms 75:4 NKJV)**

The second side of pride is character pride. It is becoming or dignified sense of what is due to oneself or one's position or character. It is self-respect and self-esteem. This side of pride produces excellence in appearance, in work ethic, and in finishing what was started; this involves character and integrity. This person will take pride in their commitments by doing what they said they would do.

And, number three is civic pride. This is the pleasure or satisfaction taken in something done by or belonging to oneself or believed to reflect credit upon oneself. In other words, this is taking pride in faith, in accomplishments, in church, etc.

Anger and Bitterness

Anger is the concrete that builds the house of bitterness. And, bitterness is the result of holding on to anger until it is impossible to forgive. Anger is a strong feeling of displeasure and belligerence aroused by a wrong perpetrated while bitterness is a feeling of antagonism, hostility, or resentfulness.

Anger can become a wall that prevents the mind from receiving and it forces others to stay away. Left to itself, anger will destroy the person who harbors it as well as those who are victims of it. Hatred, or anger, is the proof a person is carrying pain. In this case, it is important to develop an attitude that, "God will take care of this situation." Ephesians 4:26 states, *"Be angry, and do not sin": do not let the sun go down on your wrath (anger)."* When a person goes to bed nursing offense, it opens the door for anger to plant the seed of bitterness in their spirit.

Turn Bitter into Better

One letter, the letter "I," separates these two words. "I" can decide whether I stay bitter or get better; this letter can work for or against anyone. A person who is self-absorbed lives for "I." But, "I" can also mean taking responsibility for one's actions. It is in a person's power to decide if they will be a victim or if they will live in joy. "I" is the one who can prevent offenses from taking root; "I" is the deciding factor. Offenses will happen but "I" determines whether to be better or bitter.

There are many ways people get wounded. Unfortunately, husbands have left wives holding all the responsibilities including children and bills; parents have abused and neglected their children; friends have betrayed friends; spouses have committed adultery; murder has invaded people's lives; etc. The truth is, living life is the playground for woundedness; and pain presents the opportunity to nurse anger. And, to put trust in people is to expect disappointment. Remember, *"Wounded people leak issues! Hurting people hurt people! And, Healthy people heal people!"* If not dealt with, anger will kill any chance for God's blessing. It will tear down every good thing and open the door to additional problems including bitterness, lack of trust, fear, worry, perception problems, strife, gossip, pride, insecurity, inability to love others, loneliness, and many other things. It is imperative, when these things strike, to forgive immediately. Repentance and forgiveness will cause favor to flow again.

Chapter 8

Hindrances
to
Favor

The equation for peace and favor are completely different and favor is rarely studied or analyzed. Everything has a system, therefore, when the system is discovered, the path to accelerated success is found.

Favor is the shortcut to uncommon:

- Success
- Increase
- Access

Favor:

- Eliminates years of pain
- Gives someone, in a day, what it takes for another to do in a lifetime
- The currency for money
- Is explainable; it is not a mystery
- The reward for conduct
- The reward for appropriate behavior

Acts, chapter four, describes four types of favor: 1) Common, 2) Special, 3) Redemptive, and 4) Mega.

Divine favor flows through the earth as the seed for change. It is important to understand, God shows His approval through a measure of favor. Luke 2:52 states, *"And Jesus increased in wisdom and stature, and in favor with God and men."* Favor is essential for success; it is not luck, or chance, so favor must never be trivialized. It is also important to understand, the unfavored cannot help anyone to be a success. So, do not look to them for help.

People protect what they value. When introduced to favor, remember to protect the source. Favor can move a person from obscurity to greatness in a day, therefore, the source is of immense importance to their future. And it is up to the person to decide the flow of favor they will receive. Time is not relevant nor does prayer decide favor, however, asking opens the door. *I prophesy: The distance to the next supernatural wave of favor will be shortened; it will happen quickly and swiftly for the kingdom of God.*

The Palace is searching for trained behavior!

"Then the king ordered Ashpenaz, chief of his court officials, to bring into the king's service some of the Israelites from the royal family and the nobility - 4) <u>young men without any physical defect, handsome, showing aptitude for every kind of learning, well informed, quick to understand, and qualified to serve in the king's palace.</u> He was to teach them the language and literature of the Babylonians..." **(Daniel 1:3-5 NIV)**

Ashpenaz was given instructions to bring servants, with certain attributes, into the king's service to be trained according to their customs. These servants came from the royal families and nobility, of the land of Judah, which had been captured by Nebuchadnezzar, the King of Babylon. It took months for them to travel hundreds of miles, through the desert, from Judah to Babylon. Though they, most likely, walked the entirety of the trip, the servants Ashpenaz would choose, obviously, maintained their dignity and posture along the way. Now, they would be trained to live and serve in the palace of Babylon's King.

"Find me the best of the best," was Ashpenaz's assignment; he was to make sure they fit the King's list of guidelines. He was only to bring them to Nebuchadnezzar after they had been mentored in palace protocol and palace demeanor. And he was to ensure they knew how to enter the presence of a King. When three-years had ended, they had their audience with Nebuchadnezzar, King of Babylon.

Now, switch this scene unto today. Would people train for three-years to serve in their local church? Sadly, probably not. Yet, the church is the courtyard of our King's palace. The Body of Christ has been instructed to enter His gates with thanksgiving and His courts with praise. Why? Because, where they gather in His name, He is also there; the Father, Son, and Holy Spirit join the Body for worship.

Ashpenaz's servants-to-be endured all their training to learn how to protect the atmosphere and presence of a King. It is important to understand how to be in a King's presence as well as being aware of its dangers; people can lose their lives by speaking one wrong word, making one wrong sound, or having the wrong posture (attitude). Today, the Federal Bureau of Investigation trains their officers to understand the power of atmosphere, or environment. As an example, every crime scene must be protected because the evidence could be contaminated otherwise. The crime scene is the atmosphere being protected. Presence is tangible; it is a felt imprinting in an intangible world. Upon entering a room, it is possible, to discern, that people had recently been arguing there. Or, to know that someone had been there. I have been in meetings where I could tell people, in the room, had a problem and were upset. They did not have to say a word, the atmosphere carried their thoughts and emotions.

But Daniel resolved not to defile himself with the royal food and wine, and he asked the chief official for permission not to

defile himself this way. ⁹ Now God had caused the official to show favor and compassion to Daniel, ¹⁰ but the official told Daniel, "I am afraid of my lord the king, who has assigned your[c] food and drink. Why should he see you looking worse than the other young men your age? The king would then have my head because of you."

¹¹ Daniel then said to the guard whom the chief official had appointed over Daniel, Hananiah, Mishael and Azariah, ¹² "Please test your servants for ten days: Give us nothing but vegetables to eat and water to drink. ¹³ Then compare our appearance with that of the young men who eat the royal food and treat your servants in accordance with what you see." ¹⁴ So he agreed to this and tested them for ten days. ¹⁵ At the end of the ten days they looked healthier and better nourished than any of the young men who ate the royal food. ¹⁶ So the guard took away their choice food and the wine they were to drink and gave them vegetables instead.

¹⁸ At the end of the time set by the king to bring them into his service, the chief official presented them to Nebuchadnezzar. ¹⁹ The king talked with them, and he found nonequal to Daniel, Hananiah, Mishael and Azariah; so, they entered the king's service. ²⁰ In every matter of wisdom and understanding about which the king questioned them, he found them ten times better than all the magicians and enchanters in his whole kingdom. (**Daniel 1:8-20 NIV**)

In these passages, Daniel was asking for favor in regard to abstaining from eating and drinking the King's delicacies; and, instead, allowing him, and his friends, to eat and drink what they had been accustomed to. God put it in the heart of the chief official to show Daniel favor and compassion. And, though

Ashpenaz feared what the king would do, he granted his request. The result showed they were ten-times better than all the magicians and enchanters in the whole kingdom.

To these four young men God gave knowledge and understanding of all kinds of literature and learning. And Daniel could understand visions and dreams of all kinds. (Daniel 1:17 NIV)

I believe there are seven-decisions Daniel, Hananiah, Mishael, and Azariah made that enabled them to increase with promotion and favor while in the enemy's palace. Notice their location was not in a luxury suite on a secluded beach. However, that did not stop God's favor from reaching them. No matter where hell has planted the person, His favor will always provide for incredible prosperity.

Decision 1 – Fear God

To fear God is not about being afraid of Him but of knowing who He is; it is honor and putting Him first. Proverbs 9:10 states, *"The fear of the Lord is the beginning of wisdom, and knowledge of the Holy One is understanding."* Daniel honored God when he decided to challenge the chief official regarding the unclean food choices being offered them. He did this because it was Israelite custom to eat what God deemed clean rather than eat what He classified as unclean. By eating clean food, Daniel was convinced God would make them healthier than the others, otherwise, they would eat the food sacrificed to idols. As a result, God gave them powerful favor and, as it turned out, they were truly healthier and ten-times greater than the rest. The proof of fearing God is obedience.

Therefore, it is important to make knowing God's laws an obsession.

Signs of the Lack of Fear:

- Speaking ill, or wrongly, of others
- Inconsistency in church attendance
- Unwilling to tithe or give
- Being comfortable in wrong conversations, relationships, or actions
- Treating uncommon as common
- Wanting God to favor wrong actions
- Calling good evil and evil good
- Put individual will above God's

Causes for Lack of Fear:

- Perverted message of grace
- Lack of teaching regarding the finality of disobedience
- Refusing to teach about the judgment for sin
- Replacing the teaching of hell with hyper-grace

Because man is not born with the fear of God, they must be taught. It is the same with honor, they must be trained. And, with proper training on honor and integrity, people will be loyal.

Decision 2 – Stay in the Field of Favor

It is unfortunate, people can lose favor because of leaving a place too soon. Stay where there is favor; but leave when it stops. Do not be confused, when God is moving a person into another season, He will allow famine and drought in the present. Why? Because He intends to take them into a greater season of provision which is established after the present season has ended. Remember, never leave a season of favor until God has given the instruction to do so. (Read 1 Kings 17)

Ruth Stayed in the Field of Favor

To find a field of favor, it is necessary to have a mentor. Ruth had that with Naomi; she discerned the voice of favor and decided to continue with her into unfamiliar territory. Naomi was a marred and wounded person. However, Ruth looked past that and saw the hidden treasure she carried. And, now that Ruth is connected to a mentor, she will be exposed to a new nation, a new culture, and new ideas. Though her current circumstances looked devastating, she is being set up for a greater season. Nobody enjoys going through loss or pain but, sadly, it is inevitable. On the bright side, there is confidence in knowing that God will always move people forward. For Naomi, Ruth, and Orpah, their tragedy was real; they all became widows. Naomi lost her husband, as well as her sons. And, she no longer had a way to support herself or her son's widows who were looking to her for answers. I am sure, because of these very real and mind-numbing circumstances, Naomi wanted to lay down and quit. She wanted to give-up. But she did not because she was very aware of her family's need for security.

Now, unknown to Naomi, one of her daughters-in-law had destiny attached to her and would need to be mentored. This will lead Ruth to her field of favor. It is amazing how God hides treasure so that people can utilize it to find the favor He intended for them to have.

The Key! Discern, discover, attach, unlock, walk with, and overcome feelings in order to stay connected to favor.

Naomi, Ruth, and Orpah are connected to each other, and one is carrying destiny within her. Together, they all have destiny, but it will be necessary to unlock what has been hidden in the one. It is interesting to note, God never spoke to either Ruth, or Orpah, to follow, listen, or honor Naomi. However, their future is hidden in their willingness to stay connected to Naomi.

In order to identify personal fields of favor, it is necessary to go through a season of pain, loss, or even death. During this time, learn to discern who is carrying what is needed for the next season of promotion. Remember, the Bible does not say that God gave Ruth the instruction to follow Naomi. So, pay attention. Ruth determined to trust the process of mentorship rather than the security of her past. She decided she was not going to go backwards but, instead, make Naomi's future, her future. This included making Naomi's God, her God; and Naomi's people, her people. In today's modern-day, hyper grace church, people are not being asked to give up their old lifestyle for a better future.

Never Allow Feelings to Decide Your Future

Though Ruth made the right decision, it would be very difficult leaving all that was familiar to her. To make matters worse, she is now connected to a person whose name means, bitter. Even if Ruth needed confirmation that she had made the right decision, the one person who could give that to her, Orpah, was leaving. Naomi's season of losing her husband, as well as her sons, was full of pain; she left Judah full but now, she is empty. At this point, she is not capable of giving Ruth the assurance she needs about their journey. She is so broken, she instructs Ruth and Orpah to stop calling her Naomi, but Mara!

"Don't call me Naomi," she told them. "Call me Mara, because the Almighty has made my life very bitter. (Ruth 1:20 NIV)

To, successfully, find one's field of favor, it will be necessary to push past the need to be accepted. Instead of relying on feelings, decide, then stick to it. The real test comes in knowing, a person is not connected to a mentor, so they feel they belong. However, they are connected to train them to belong to their future.

Areas People Wrestle with Change:

- Allowing the old man to die
- Being real while embracing the new man
- Having a teachable mind for a better future

Fields of favor come with the price of enduring a season of training. Instead of allowing feelings to get in the way, look for every nugget of knowledge and apply it. Then, once connected to a mentor, learn how to stay connected; without making the necessary changes, favor could be lost. It is important to know, God is not obligated to give second chances. So, make every effort to acquire the mentality necessary to pay the price of staying in the field of favor.

Kingdom Consistency and the Price of Favor includes:

- Order
- Instruction
- Obedience
- Honor
- Favor

- Finishing

Training and instruction always bring about order; they are the test that activates obedience. And obedience is the qualification for more. Therefore, God will trust people with the hidden riches of secret places as His divine word, laws, principles, and commands are followed.

"I will give you the treasures of darkness and hidden riches of secret places, that you may know that I, the LORD, who call you by your name, Am the God of Israel." **(Isaiah 45:3 NKJV)**

However, where there is dishonor, obedience is lacking; on the other hand, where there is honor, there is favor. And, with His favor, people become finishers. Starting is great, growing is better, but finishing is the essence of being empowered by Holy Spirit. My question becomes, "What good is starting if you can't finish?" I have witnessed many great starters but few finishers. Remember, when it comes to walking in favor, feelings are the number one enemy. They produce emotions that can rob people of their field of favor.

Decision 3 – Show Honor

To attain a field of favor, it becomes important to extend honor to the one who holds the information which will move an individual out of their season of pain. The world is full of dishonor; and honor does not mean agreeing with someone's lifestyle. Nor does it mean agreeing with everything they say or believe. Honor simply means to understand the law of protocol and respect. For parents, God makes this clear in the Bible.

Honor can make the difference between the present and the future. Most people learn obedience at the threat of loss, or pain, but few are taught the law of honor. Honor is from another world and shows up in one's tone of voice, or in their countenance. Honor caused Pharoah to make Joseph second in command, in all of Egypt. (Genesis 41) In the book of Esther, Queen Vashti lost her position due to dishonoring King Ahasuerus. (Esther 1:12-19) Nearly every loss in life comes because of dishonor. Wouldn't it be nice if people could pluck up every seed of dishonor sown? Clearly, there is no room, nor excuse, for dishonor. Even if a person does another person dirty, there is not a scripture that approves of dishonoring that person. Also, attraction is not proof of honor. Telling someone, "I love you," does not mean honor. But honor is proven through a person's actions not by their words. So, do not only listen for honor, look for it as well. A person's future can be predicted based on how they extend honor, not their resume. A resume is a list of past accomplishments and work history but not attitude or character. Lucifer served God. He had a great resume; however, he dishonored Him by declaring his intention of taking His throne.

By learning honor, access is available in any environment on earth. Honor is the seed that guarantees access; it is high respect. Honor places value on the differences of others. Usually, honor does not come naturally, it must be taught. So, I encourage the training of all children. And reward them when honor is acted out rather than when they are being cute. Lack of honor is, generally, the root of most relational problems.

- Honor is a bridge
- Honor creates a memory
- Honor is currency

With honor, it is possible to make up for what is lacking. Honor is not a gift from God. However, it is a decision to value someone, or something; it is a chosen virtue. Truly, it is an act of wisdom to kill the snake of dishonor. And, to get a picture of dishonor, watch the news media, or talk shows. This industry thrives off dishonoring the virtues of others. Sadly, what does this say about what their audience expects? Honor is revealed protocol and is revealed through body language. It is the most important currency on earth and can be lost in one moment of dishonor. Do not let a day ruin what took twenty-years to build.

Abraham had many flaws, so, why did God continue to bless him? I believe it was because he knew how to honor Him. Without a doubt, all people make mistakes; however, it is each person's, individual, responsibility to learn the law of honor. By doing this it can, potentially, turn a life around in twenty-four hours. Unfortunately, anyone can see, dishonor is always on display in the United States; no wonder this country is in such a mess. It would be nice if people understood, the seed of dishonor creates loss. On the other hand, honor is a powerful wealth key. Daily, consider questioning how to honor God, and people. Then, upon recognizing dishonor, ask forgiveness. Honor has proven to be the greatest quality to be trusted.

- Honor authority
- Honor God's presence
- Honor your parents
- Honor your Husband/Wife

Decision 4 – Be a Problem Solver

Problem solvers attract favor because of their quick and accurate response as well as their effectiveness. The difference between the wealthy and the poor is inspiration and infuriation;

one is eager to solve the problem and the other is angry because there is a problem.

People are either remembered by the problems they solve or the problems they create. The question is, "Do I solve problems, or create them?" Whatever the case, people were placed on earth to be problem solvers. Once it is recognized, problem solvers become more valuable to themselves and others. Afterall, it is necessary to recognize problems, but the greater asset is figuring out the solution.

Determining to help others solve their problems qualifies that individual for Psalms 65:11-12.

You crown the year with your bounty, and your carts overflow with abundance. 12) The grasslands of the wilderness overflow; the hills are clothed with gladness. **(NIV)**

Decision 5 – Sow Seed

Sowing seed is one of the greatest, biblical, laws; and, once unlocked, being broke will never be an option again. Everything required for the future is contained within a seed. And, according to Genesis 8:22, *"As long as the earth remains, seed time and harvest will not cease."* In the natural world, there is a season to sow and, that season, will determine the timing of the harvest. However, it is completely different in the Kingdom of God; the seed determines the season. When understood, this is powerful. Seed does not have to wait on a particular season, it decides the season.

1 Kings 3:3-14; Matthew 26: 7-13

The RIGHT Seed Gets God's Attention

The RIGHT seed is a transitional seed that is planted between the gaps of seasons. Here are some facts on the Right Seed:

- Will get God's attention
- Will attract Satanic warfare
- Will link you to a man of God
- Will authorize divine promotion
- Will unlock new seasons
- Will require uncommon obedience
- Will be a portrait of faith

There are requirements to sowing the right seed. The first includes discerning the correct soil. Without soil, the seed is useless; it will not produce anything. Without the "right" soil, the seed has no identity, nor can it reveal its assignment. Soil really does matter. Jesus, in Matthew, Mark, Luke, and John, spoke about four conditions of the ground and how the seed reacted to each one.

- Hard soil, or falling by the wayside, conditions prevent the seed from entering the earth. Therefore, the birds devour the seed.
- Rocky soil is shallow. Though the seed springs up, it has no depth, and the sun scorches it. And, for lack of a good root system, it dies.
- The thorn bushes, on thorny soil, choke the seed so that it cannot grow.
- Good ground yields a harvest from the seed – it could be a hundredfold, sixty-fold, or thirty-fold more than the seed.

Seed Facts:

1. Seed is God-Directed; therefore, it is necessary to be sensitive to His voice to know which covenant seed is required for the miracle needed.
2. Faith is a necessity so make sure it is proportionate to the dream.
3. King David said, *"I will not offer unto God something that cost me nothing."* (2 Samuel 2:24 NKJV) Seed is costly; it is precious.
4. Again, seed requires faith. It determines divine timing and can accelerate a seed's growth.
5. Seeds are photographs of a person's faith, or an expectation of a harvest.

Faith Facts:

1. Faith is substance and hope. *"Faith is the substance of things hoped for..."* (Hebrews 11:1 NKJV)
2. Faith pleases God. *"But without faith it is impossible to please Him..."* (Hebrews 11:6 NKJV)
3. Faith is given to everyone. *"...God has dealt to each one a measure of faith."* (Romans 12:3)
4. Faith grants access to God. *"...through whom also we have access by faith into this grace in which we stand..."* (Romans 5:2 NKJV)
5. Faith justifies. *"...a man is justified by faith..."* (Romans 3:28 NKJV)
6. Faith comes by hearing. *"So, then faith comes by hearing, and hearing by the word of God."* (Romans 10:17 NKJV)

Decision 6 – Reward Favor

Because appreciation is a seed, be conscientious of celebrating those who extend their favor. Being thankful is a wealth key for success and, as a seed, carries tremendous power within it. And, to prevent the feeling of being taken advantage of, practice the art of receiving. Remember, favor is attracted to gracious, or grateful, receivers.

When being mentored, it is a good idea to refrain from opening the door wider than what was intended. Earlier in my ministry, I was given access to an incredibly, wealthy businessman. Due to lack of wisdom, I would bring a friend every time we met; I thought my friend needed his mentorship as much as I did. However, the businessman informed me, *"Just because I have given you access into my world, doesn't mean that I have given it to your friend."* At this revelation, I was horrified and somewhat embarrassed. As a result of being kind to my friend, I almost lost the access I had been given. Without a doubt, it can be very costly to force the door open wider than what is permitted. Therefore, always remember the law of protocol in the presence of a mentor.

Decision 7 – Honor the Command to Tithe

An evil philosophy will introduce error, discredit truth, and discredit the source of truth. For example, overtime, the truth regarding the tithe has been discredited. But, in truth, it is a heavenly key that can unlock the window to His divine world of plenty. Tithing is not a church gimmick to manipulate money from people, it is a command from God. Malachi 3:10 states, *"Bring all the tithes into the storehouse, that there may be food in My house..."* Therefore, it is a measuring rod God uses to determine His divine portion. Continuing in verse 10, He says, *"And try Me now in this, says the Lord of hosts, if I will not open for you the windows of heaven and pour out for you such*

131

blessing that there will not be room enough to receive it." This is the promise that follows the command; do what He says and have an overflowing blessing in return. What an amazing test of God's faithfulness. This is not a matter of getting what is wanted or receiving what has been prayed for; He only gives a person what they can manage. And, it is easy to manage the tithe because it is ten cents of every dollar. However, the hard part is releasing it to the Source of all things who owns it. Why would God say, in Malachi 3:8, He is being robbed of the tithe if it did not already belong to Him? So, in neglecting to follow this commandment, God cannot trust people with the other ninety cents of that dollar. Remember, the tithe is a key to the window of God's promises.

"For I am the Lord, I do not change; therefore, you are not consumed, O sons of Jacob. 7) Yet from the days of your fathers you have gone away from My ordinances and have not kept them. Return to Me, and I will return to you," says the Lord of hosts. "But you said, 'In what way shall we return?' "Will a man rob God? Yet you have robbed Me! But you say, 'In what way have we robbed You?' In tithes and offerings. 9) You are cursed with a curse, for you have robbed Me, even this whole nation. 10) Bring all the tithes into the storehouse, that there may be food in My house, and try Me now in this," says the Lord of hosts, "if I will not open for you the windows of heaven and pour out for you such blessing that there will not be room enough to receive it. 11) "And I will rebuke the devourer for your sakes, so that he will not destroy the fruit of your ground, nor shall the vine fail to bear fruit for you in the field," says the Lord of hosts; 12) "And all nations will call you blessed, for you will be a delightful land," says the Lord of hosts. (Malachi 3:6-12 NKJV)

Chapter 9

Favor Plows
Forward
Not Back

So, Elijah went from there and found Elisha, son of Shaphat. He was plowing with twelve yoke of oxen, and he himself was driving the twelfth pair. Elijah went up to him and threw his cloak around him. 20) Elisha then left his oxen and ran after Elijah. "Let me kiss my father and mother good-by," he said, "and then I will come with you."

"Go back," Elijah replied. "What have I done to you?"
(1 Kings 19:19-20 NIV)

Let me paint a picture on how I see this whole story...

It was a hot day; the air was cloudy, and it was hard to breathe because of the dust from the freshly, plowed fields. The young man, who was guiding the oxen, was tired as he had worked all day; he had a deadline for preparing the ground for new seed. And, the season for sowing was rapidly approaching. Therefore, Elisha had been working long, hard days to meet this deadline. As the owner of the property, it was his responsibility to get the seed in the ground before the window of opportunity, for sowing, would close. Elisha not only owned the land, but he owned twelve-yoke of oxen plus the plows. He joined with the other laborers to prepare the fields.

Elisha built his plowing business early in life, but as time progressed, he seems to have lost his passion. However, on one day, it was not a routine plowing day, because the outcome was unlike the rest. One can imagine how Elisha would drift into daydreaming mode while working to maintain straight furrows behind the plow. He could have been wondering why he was unfulfilled, or stuck, while having tremendous potential for more. During this time, he was trying to make sense of his life. He believed he was stuck in a rut, or in a dull and unpromising future. At this place, for him, being thankful and full of joy was hard. After all, no one, in his village, had accomplished as much in such a short period of time. Sadly, as he looked back at the other plowmen, he noticed they were laughing and enjoying their success; but he was asking himself, *"What is wrong with me?"* His tears, landing onto the dry fields, only accentuated his unfulfilled life.

Like so many, Elisha was asking himself, *"What am I going to do with the rest of my life? Is this all there is, working behind the butt of an ox? Will I ever see more of this world?"* Though he had accomplished much, he still felt the weight of the potential placed within him; for, God will not allow satisfaction, or money, to override a greater purpose. Elisha knew, in his heart, there was more to life than following an ox with a plow. A gnawing feeling would always remind him he could be doing something more. And, unfortunately, most people do not understand this type of drive. As a matter of fact, many will believe this to be crazy. Could it be, Elisha thought he was crazy as well.

Though the ox was strong and, with great ease, could pull an extreme amount of weight, it was also dumb. Many people, along with Elisha, have metaphorically been plowing behind dumb things for long enough. Dumb things, and decisions, can weigh a person down with multiple problems and heartaches. Right now, the world is full of people who hate the lives they are living and would like to have a do over. This time, though, making the right decisions where, previously, they had made wrong ones. Too bad that is, usually, not possible; however, learning from mistakes is a preventative for a better tomorrow. For now, discover the "dumb" thing that precipitated the consequences of today and then, implement better decisions in order to achieve greatness in the future.

The truth of the matter is that everyone has made dumb, or stupid, decisions that cost them greatly. Most people could ask themselves, *"What went wrong?"* And, for those who ask and then, fight depression and failure, they will eventually climb out of that pit in order to conquer the decisions of their past. If, at some point, life begins to seem unfulfilling, it might be the inner voice of the spirit whispering, *"There's more to life than an ox and a plow."* It could be the tug of a greater potential, or the feeling of labor pains prior to delivery.

Unfortunately, life can become mundane, or unimaginative. Life can be like the plow which digs up dirt day after day after day. It is repeatedly doing the same thing, every day, with the added frustration of dealing with the rocks, stones, and roots that show up in the process. It is having to fight the hard soil of life while lacking interest or excitement. Elisha could very well end up like this if something does not change. Though he was not doing anything wrong, he was fed up with his present. Destiny was calling his name and God was preparing him for the entrance of a "father," or a mentor.

Now, what about Elijah, the prophet of God? He was at a place called Beersheba, in Judah, depressed, worn out, and wishing he were dead. Why? He had just called down the fire of God on Mount Carmel and he killed over four-hundred false prophets of Baal, in one of the greatest showdowns in the bible. Then, after praying seven-times, he ended a three-year drought which he prophesied would take place.

Elijah went before the people and said, "How long will you waver between two opinions? If the LORD is God, follow him; but if Baal is God, follow him." But the people said nothing. 22) Then Elijah said to them, "I am the only one of the LORD's prophets left, but Baal has four hundred and fifty prophets. 23) Get two bulls for us. Let them choose one for themselves and let them cut it into pieces and put it on the wood but not set fire to it. I will prepare the other bull and put it on the wood but not set fire to it. 24) Then you call on the name of your god, and I will call on the name of the LORD. The god who answers by fire-he is God." **(1 Kings 18:21 NIV)**

In the end, after Elijah addressed the God of Abraham, Isaac, and Jacob, the fire of the Lord fell, then, the four-hundred and fifty prophets of Baal, fell as well. Afterwards, Queen Jezebel, King Ahab's wife, declared to Elijah, *"May the gods deal with me, be it ever so severely, if by this time tomorrow I do not make your life like that of one of them (the false prophets Elijah killed)."* Out of fear, Elijah ran for his life. This is crazy; he had the faith to call down fire on a watered-down altar but lacked the faith to face Jezebel.

3) Elijah was afraid and ran for his life. When he came to Beersheba in Judah, he left his servant there, 4) while he himself went a day's journey into the desert. He came to a broom tree, sat down under it and prayed that he might die. "I have had enough, LORD," he said. "Take my life; I am no better than my ancestors." 5) Then he lay down under the tree and fell asleep. (1 Kings 19:3-5 NIV)

Elijah was no ordinary prophet; he was the chief of all the prophets. He was also the leader of the school of prophets. So, what happened? According to him, *"I have had enough, Lord."* He was tired of fighting King Ahab and Queen Jezebel. He was exhausted from taking three-steps forward and two-steps back.

All at once an angel touched him and said, "Get up and eat." 6) He looked around, and there by his head was a cake of bread baked over hot coals, and a jar of water. He ate and drank and then lay down again. 7) The angel of the LORD came back a

137

second time and touched him and said, "Get up and eat, for the journey is too much for you." 8) So he got up and ate and drank. Strengthened by that food, he traveled forty days and forty nights until he reached Horeb, the mountain of God. 9) There he went into a cave and spent the night. (1 Kings 19:5-9 NIV)

How did Elijah get to this dark, and dreary, place? Jezebel never laid a hand on him; all she did was make a threat against this man of God. However, her words were capable of doing more damage than most physical attacks. It can take years, and up to a lifetime, to heal verbal wounds while physical wounds can heal in a few, short weeks. And, verbal threats are internalized which makes them harder to overcome. Elijah ended up in a cave because he allowed the enemy to mess with his mind with a lie. The lie became bigger than the truth; Jezebel would never be able to get close enough to carry out her threat. Why? God had plans for Elijah to father a spiritual son.

Unfortunately, life has a way of driving people into the cave of despair and depression. Therefore, with all diligence, stay out of the cave of isolation. Caves produce tunnel vision and cause a narrow focus directed on problems rather than solutions. Satan would love to shove people into caves of fear, regret, lack, and doubt; but, if he can get people into isolation, and they remain there, it will prevent them from ever moving forward. Elijah was in such a cave and began losing his purpose for life because of focusing on his problems. By being consumed with present circumstances, it is easy to lose focus on what is important in life. Desperation is not a good thing.

It is true, God anoints people for ministry, however, He anoints them alongside their weaknesses. And, He allows those weaknesses to remain in order to prevent people from getting lost in their "works" and, then, forgetting the One in whom they serve. While Elijah was hiding from the threats of his nemesis, God begins painting a picture that, beyond his present situation, reveals his future. God speaks to him regarding Elisha, his predecessor and then, tells him to, *"Go, return on your way to the Wilderness of Damascus...And Elisha the son of Shaphat of Abel Meholah you shall anoint as prophet in your place."* (1 Kings 19:15-16 NKJV) Now, through the still small voice, Elijah has direction. However, it took the cave for him to realize, he needed to look beyond the storm, his present situation, in order to focus on the future contained in God's plan.

In obedience, Elijah departs from the cave and finds Elisha, casting his mantle upon him. This was a crossroads for both Elijah and Elisha; one had questions while the other had answers. It is here, at the crossroads of life, that greatness is forged, and transfer takes place. This is where the "Paul's" transform the "Timothy's," the "Jonathan's" transform the "David's," and the "Naomi's" transform the "Ruth's." And, it is important to pay attention to those met in the crossroads of life. They could be the ones who can change a person's wrong focus and then, are able to move them out of the ordinary and into the extraordinary. Here the questions and answers come together in power to do what was, previously, impossible.

Imagine Elisha's frustration when he saw Elijah walking across his freshly plowed fields. I wonder if he was thinking, *"What is this crazy, old man doing out here? Doesn't he understand, I have a schedule to keep? Now, I must clean up his mess too."* Maybe, Elisha thought he had messed up his work; and, maybe, this caused him to reflect on all the messes he has spent his lifetime trying to clean up. Perhaps, Elijah stirred up everything Elisha thought he had hidden and caused him to see what he did not, really, want to see. It, possibly, brought to his attention, again, how he was stuck in an unimaginative place in life. Now, in this place, would he allow another person to challenge him to change?

The first step for change is by allowing God to step into the middle of the current, life's work and dreams. This is for the purpose of creating, or igniting, the person's future. And, when this happens, it will take place in the way lest expected. So, do not be scared; recognize, though it may have messed up a picture-perfect day, it is necessary to break up the rut of life. Therefore, get excited when destiny is walking on top of a freshly plowed life. In the end, it will not be regretted.

When Elisha faces Elijah he states, *"Please let me kiss my father and my mother, and then I will follow you."* Elijah's response was, *"Go back again, for what have I done to you?"* Then, Elisha did a powerful thing, he destroyed his ability to return to plowing the fields. He slaughtered his oxen, cooked it on a fire made from his equipment, then gave it to the people to eat. Elijah must have been wondering what had gotten into this young man. However, Elisha wanted to burn the bridge of temptation. He did not want to return to a dead-end job when things got tough. Or, when he got frustrated and angry with his spiritual father. Elisha understood that favor would take him anywhere but "back."

Following the call of God is never easy and, if people say that it is, I question the sincerity of their call. There are some, with very little training, who come to me believing they are called to the ministry but, then, complain when asked to serve. They say things like, *"I am anointed to preach; I am called to the platform; or, God has bigger things for me."* The truth is, *"if a person is not willing to do the small things, they will never be allowed to do the greater things."*

If a Person Will not be Corrected, He Cannot be Connected

To walk in favor, people must be willing to learn, and be corrected, at the feet of a spiritual father. One such man is, Bishop Joby Brady. As a spiritual father, he will tell a ministry when anything is out of place or if something is wrong for that house. So, when encountering a prophet who is willing to help, allow them to walk over your freshly plowed fields; that is why they are there. By accepting their correction, a connection is established with God. Remember, "Correction is connection!"

Favor is more than money, or materialism, it is the power of access. It is the ability to move into the influence of another who can add information, wisdom, and ideas for the purpose of increase. For growth, two are always better than one. Therefore, men need fathers for identity as well as for knowledge and impartation. Favor results in serving someone who is already favored. As a mentor is served, the favor upon his life will, eventually, be extended. This will bring about the desired growth in the life of the one who serves.

It is good to be noticed because the right person can help others get promoted. This makes access more powerful than money. As God applies His seal of approval, favor comes, thereby enabling others to notice; this moves a questioning person to serve under their leadership. And, it is a good indication of favor when a person finds themselves with people, and in places, they ordinarily would not be. Favor is the vehicle that will bring about a faster promotion and will change a lifestyle from mundane to extraordinary.

Elisha began questioning his life and Elijah favored him with the answers. However, even with the right mentor helping and guiding their new students, making changes is not easy. Elisha had a security blanket with his business so, I am sure, walking away was not the top thing on his "to do" list. Following the call of God is hard, but faith is built up as people overcome bad situations in life. Favor and faith are cousins. And, the favor of God will come as someone steps into territory that is unfamiliar. This can look like a sea of darkness while hearing the voice of God say, *"Come."* In Matthew, chapter fourteen, Peter did this. At Jesus' command, while the storm was raging, he walked on water. Favor will not leave those who step into dark, unfamiliar places. With favor, everything will be okay. However, if a person is not sent, or called, by the Word of God, favor will not go.

Elisha's next steps would not be easy. Faith would require him to completely, step out on the Word of God. He would have to believe, and rely on, His Word to walk away from everything he has always known. Here, good men are born into greatness. And, if they are willing to continue trusting Him until He promotes them, they will accomplish great things.

Elisha is no longer self-employed; He works for the Source of all things. To the immature, it is assumed, this "job" will be easy and full of rewards. The truth is, rewards do come, however, not without tests and trials. This is because, God will not give what people cannot be trusted with. And, in order to live the life of a king, people must first learn to live the life of a servant. In this, timing will be their greatest asset. And, instead of comparing themselves with others, it is better to discern when their timing is at hand. Remember, *"Timing is the hinge the door of favor hangs on and faith is the key that unlocks the door. While, giving is the power that forces the door of favor open."* And, when favor is opened, the harvest will come. Again, *"Favor begins as a seed then it produces a harvest."*

Favor is a Seed Before it is a Harvest

Elisha went from plowing in his owns fields, to spiritual plowing in another. He spent the next fifteen-years pouring water on Elijah's hands; or serving his needs. In the natural, it looked as though he was just a servant, however, God saw him as one who would minister through His anointing. Throughout his training period, Elisha will be transformed into the man who, when the timing was right, could carry the anointing that rested on Elijah. His service to Elijah was preparing him to serve others spiritually.

At this level of servanthood, with determination, insignificant people become significant and ordinary people become extraordinary. However, it is not always easy to maintain the right attitude. I am sure, many times, Elijah and Elisha had differences of opinion as well as some rough times. There were probably hard days, sad moments, and silent questions they had to manage during Elisha's training. I imagine some of Elisha's questions were, *"Have I done the right thing? When will I be released into ministry? Why is this taking so long?"* However, he buries his feelings and stays in the attitude of a good protégé.

As a mentor, it is a good idea to know the difference between a parasite and a protégé; one adds to while the other takes away. To distinguish between the two, look for correctability. Do not connect to a person who refuses to be corrected.

Protégé, or apprentice, is a person under the patronage, protection, or care of someone interested in his or her career or welfare. (Dictionary.com)

- Wants to learn from his mentor
- Wants to gain their mentor's knowledge
- Thinks about their mentor's well-being
- Will always offer to serve their mentor
- Adds to their mentor's joy

Parasite, or freeloader, is a person who receives support, advantage, or the like, from another without giving any useful return; he lives on the hospitality of others. (Dictionary.com)

- Wants to take from their mentor
- Wants to dispute their mentor's knowledge
- Always thinks about themselves
- Has a "what about me" attitude
- Takes away their mentor's joy

As a protégé, Elisha knew when to speak and, more importantly, when to listen. He was able to make the transition from plowing to pouring; something most people are not able to do. However, transition is the key to the entry of the next season. Without this happening, success does not happen either. And, it is necessary to discern the code of conduct for the next season, otherwise, the present season could become permanent. As an example, the military is taught a code of conduct that must be adhered to even if captured. *A code of conduct is a set of rules outlining the norms, rules, and responsibilities or proper practices of an individual party or an organization.* (Wikipedia) Unfortunately, there are multitudes of men and women who will never transition beyond their present situation because they have not discovered the code of conduct necessary for the next season. The reasons are numerous. However, fear stops some from taking the leap of faith necessary; maybe the risks are too great. Then, others are stopped from seeing their future potential by anger and bitterness, due to past mistakes. Or, word curses such as, *"You will never amount to anything,"* have paralyzed them.

(At this point, I would like to encourage those reading this book, to read Dr. Mike Murdock's material on leadership.)

You Will Never Rise Above Your Self-Image

Transition is the key to unlocking the code that has been encrypted within every person's deoxyribonucleic acid, or DNA. And, behind this door, is the code to purpose. When Elisha destroyed his oxen, along with the plows, he proved he possessed the mental resources necessary to transition into his next season. This decision enabled him to focus on his future rather than looking back to his past. Burning the un-necessary bridges, of the past, is vital to walk in the favor needed for the next season. Favor can take a person anywhere but back.

Favor
- Favor is not connected to a person's abilities.
- Favor is not dependent upon a person's ability to get the job done, but the willingness to try.
- Favor looks for the willing not the gifted.
- Favor is not granted to those who possess the power of understanding, but to those who are ready to obey that understanding.

Sadly, churches are full of people who understand truth but do not operate in truth. Most attend services, going through the motions, believing they are doing something great for God. However, attending services for the purpose of getting something, rather than giving, is not God's plan.

Favor does not say, *"Well, if you have the abilities, and the time, I'll do it."* Favor does not wait on the college graduate in order to activate a person. Favor will grab people in the little, mundane activities and turn them into great things. And, because of a person's willingness to "burn their plow and cut up their oxen," favor will reach into the gutter of their life in order to pull them out. And, for the purpose of transformation, favor looks for the underdog and cheers for the insignificant. In other words, favor will drag, pull, and drive a person anywhere but backwards.

Now, if possible, look as far back to the left, then do the same on the right. Now, look forward without ever looking back again.

Today, it is time to chop up everything holding you back. So, for God to activate you, deal with the past and make peace with it; this will give you power to move into your future. No one will ever be exempt from a past full of pain, failure, woundedness, and loss; and, for some, these things will bring them close to destruction. Psalm 124:2-3 states, *"If it had not been for the Lord who was on our side, when men rose up against us, 3) then they would have swallowed us alive, etc."* Most people would have died in their mess had it not been for God helping them. Fortunately, the past has no bearing on God's plan for a person's life. And, thankfully, history does not decide destiny; for, the blood of Jesus washes the slate clean when salvation occurs. The past is forgotten and, the forgiveness of all past failures and mistakes, makes for a new and lasting future. By His stripes, He healed all wounds, and He carried all pains. Then, He guides people into, and through, their next season. Be aware, though, Satan's biggest weapon is in reminding people of their past mistakes.

Again, I am thankful God does not investigate the past to decide the future. He knows the end from the beginning. Therefore, He is always focused on what He knows to be the final, result, which is "Good." I believe it is not only time, but necessary for the body of Christ to do the same. *"Favor will take us anywhere but backwards."*

Over and Under Principle for Favor

Remember, people can never be a Chief Executive Officer, or CEO, until they have first proven themselves under a supervisor. Or, until they have proven to be a good apprentice under their mentor. It is here, in serving, God decides where, and when, to elevate a person; this is the key, the law of servanthood.

However, the principle of favor is determined by one's determination to "wait on God." And Elisha serves as an example of one who waited. As a reminder, he waited for fifteen-years before he received Elijah's mantel. Waiting is one of the greatest tests for promotion as well as proof of trust. And, timing is the power for accumulation.

*Even the youths shall faint and be weary, and the young men shall utterly fall: 31 **But they that wait upon the LORD** shall renew their strength; they shall mount up with wings as eagles; they shall run, and not be weary; and they shall walk, and not faint. (Isa 40:30-31 KJV)*

If a person's motivation is in the interests of the kingdom of God, rather than self-promotion, they will walk in a higher anointing. As an example, Elisha's process, out of the mundane, followed these steps:

- Plowing
- Pouring
- Promotion
- Performance
- Prophecy

For advancement, without rushing through the process, these are the steps all leaders should expect. Transition happens between each step making it possible to go on to the next level. However, most people are not able to make the adjustments required because it is too uncomfortable, or hard. Thus, though transition is the key to greatness and favor, many miss the mark. And remember, what took Elijah a lifetime to accomplish, Elisha was able to accomplish, in a day, because he learned how to transition. Therefore, continue to move forward, make the necessary changes, and walk with the right attitude in every valley of transition.

Favor will take over and will take us anywhere but backwards.

Foot Notes

1. Douglas, M. *Purity and danger: an analysis of concept of pollution and taboo.* (Routledge, 2005).

Made in the USA
Middletown, DE
19 September 2022